THE LUXURY OF TEARS

THE LUXURY OF TEARS

Winning Stories from the National Society of Arts and Letters Competition

Edited by Susan Marie Greenburg

August House / Little Rock
P U B L I S H E R S

Printed in the United States of America

10 9 8 7 6 5 4 3 2 1

The Luxury of tears: winning stories from the National Society of
Arts and Letters competition / edited by Susan Marie Greenburg.—
1st ed.
p.   cm.   ISBN 0-87483-093-1
1. Short stories, American.   I. Greenburg, Susan Marie.
II. National Society of Arts and Letters (U.S.)
PS648.S5L88   1989
813′.0108—dc20   89-32040 CIP

Production artwork by Ira Hocut
Project direction by Ted Parkhurst
Typography by Arrow Connection

This book is printed on archival-quality paper which meets the
guidelines for performance and durability of the Committee
on Production Guidelines for book Longevity of the Council
on Library Resources.

AUGUST HOUSE, INC.   PUBLISHERS   LITTLE ROCK

To
Victor Niiranen, National President;
National Board of Directors;
and Members of
The National Society of Arts and Letters

WITH APPRECIATION

Contents

Foreword

I began reading short stories because they were short, something that could be read in one sitting, on the school bus, during math class, or between chores. I began writing short stories for the same reason; they were short. I had been trying to write full-length plays and the short story form seemed a pleasant diversion. I expected to write a short story in a few hours or a few days. How long could it take to write two thousand words? That wasn't many more words than a sonnet.

That was before I learned the hard lessons of writing: that less is more, that length has little to do with size, and that the difference between a short story and a novel is roughly the difference between a watch and a clock tower.

Contrary to popular opinion, the short story form is not for beginning writers or beginning readers. The short story requires skill on the part of the writer, discernment on the part of the reader, and on the part of both, willingness to see beyond the obvious.

Perhaps the novel requires more arduous, sustained work over a longer period of time, more scaffolding, more bricks and a larger foundation. That was why George Sessions Perry said a short story is like a date, a novel is like a marriage. I think it would be more correct to say that a short story is a moment in a marriage that encapsulates the first thirty years—the wins, the losses, the slumps, the batting averages, the arguments with the umpires, the fights in the locker room. The short story is one brief crisis in a marriage, but in that crisis is revealed the relationship with all of its ramifications.

There is, of course, a trick to writing the short story. That trick is to introduce interesting characters and a vital problem, set the atmosphere, tone and voice of the story, fit in the background information and symbolism necessary for understanding the story, and get it all into the first paragraph. The rest of it is easier, but the first part is roughly the equivalent of compressing a baseball game into the first inning. It can be done, but you feel witness to a miracle when it happens.

Why then this collection of stories, even prize-winning stories, by young writers? These are no ordinary young people, and no ordinary writers. Their vision is not measured by the number of their days but by the insight and wisdom they have packed into those days.

In my first fumbling attempts at the short story, after days, weeks, even months of wrestling with characters that wouldn't breathe and plots that wouldn't move, I often shelved the stories because I didn't know enough to complete them. I hadn't lived long enough, or hadn't experienced enough, or didn't have enough insight into that experience to understand what I was trying to do. And if I couldn't understand it, I couldn't express it in any way that would be meaningful to the reader.

From time to time I have dragged some of those old stories from the files and looked over the yellow pages to chuckle at the brittle words and purple phrases, to blanche at the inconsistencies and the inability to deal honestly with hard emotions and painful truths, and occasionally, to discover that I had somehow learned what I needed to know to finish the story.

It requires a courageous and determined person of any age to tackle the short story, one of the most difficult and demanding forms of prose writing. These young writers are a fearless lot. They tackle the problems of the short story form and the problems of being a human being at one and the same time. And they do it with high humor, with seriousness of purpose, with dignity, with style, and with grace.

In "Dragon Lady and the Ponytail Plant," Laura Leigh Hancock writes of family relations in conflict with traditional values. Carol Vivian Spaulding deals with youth and old age, living and dying, dreaming and grieving in "Not If, When."

Two young people face fear and failure and the courage to go on in David Anthony Dobbs's "Placing Protection," and Tina Marie Conway uses the past with its losses and lessons to give meaning to the present in "World War II Picture." In Young William Smith's "Midway," the youthful narrator must choose between the failed past and the unknown present in the midst of love with all its betrayals.

None of the stories focuses on private matters and temporary concerns—the little problems of little people—but they focus on those things that concern all of us, matters of the heart and mind, human values, family, traditions, youth and old age, and of the fear and failure that diminishes but cannot dim hope. These writers are not afraid to face the problems in the human condition. Theirs is not the empty idealism of untried youth, but the courageous acceptance of outrageous fortune, the intolerance of injustice, and the honest if painful acceptance that not every problem has a solution, and of those that do, many cannot be solved in four thousand words or less.

This understanding, this courage, is even more remarkable because these are children of a nation that has been accused of sacrificing its youth to the one-eyed god. Yet these young people dare entertain through enlightenment. They challenge the reader to think and discover with them, to face unpleasant truths, to make unpopular choices. These young writers understand that amusement as an end in itself leads to surfeit, to hollow men and women, to citizens ill-equipped for the decisions required by a democracy.

These are our children. These are our citizens, and their drive to excel in a nation that rewards success rather than excellence, their energetic examination of values in a nation that is not amused by thought, their uneasy acceptance of the rights and guilts of citizenship will serve us all. And their stories will entertain and enlighten many of us.

Robert Flynn
NOVELIST IN RESIDENCE
TRINITY UNIVERSITY
SAN ANTONIO, TEXAS

Preface

The National Society of Arts and Letters was founded in 1944 in Washington, D.C., by Mollie Davis Nicholson, a writer, editor, and lecturer; and by Francesca Falk Miller Nielsen, a concert soprano, playwright, and poet. The Certificate of Incorporation described their intent in these words: ". . . to aid, assist, and sponsor young artists; to create opportunities for artistic endeavor and expression; to encourage and promote beneficial interest and development in creative art."

The National Society of Arts and Letters has never wavered from the inner vision of these two gifted women. It developed its National Career Awards concept, through which cash awards are given to winners of competitions conducted annually in one of the categories of membership: dance, art, music, literature and drama.

The 1988 National Career Awards Competition was in literature—the short story. Winners of twenty-four chapter competitions were finalists for national awards. Their manuscripts were submitted to three distinguished judges, Fletcher Knebel, prize-winning novelist; Dr. Nicholas Salerno, chairman of the department of English, Arizona State University; and Dr. John E. Hallwas, author, critic, and professor of English and Director of Regional Collections at Western Illinois University. Although the judges' scores were expressive of their individual judgments, the scoring system resulted in a clear consensus for the prize-winning short stories. Twenty of the finalists were present at Honolulu for a master class given by Pulitzer Prize–winner Leon Edel, author of the five-volume *Life of Henry James*, and for the awards ceremony, at which twelve of the young writers received cash awards totaling in excess of twenty thousand dollars.

Our National Career Awards winners go on to successful and in many cases brilliant careers. While their progress is oftan aided by career development opportunities offered by the National Society of Arts and Letters, it is the continuing interest of the sponsoring chapter that fundamentally sustains them, and continues to do so wherever in the world art or letters may take them.

In addition to the work of the literary judges, the society would like to acknowledge others without whose valuable contributions this book would not have been possible: Peggy McNamara Brown of the Austin, Texas, chapter, National President of NSAL in 1988; Eudora Welty, National Advisor; Reva Shiner of the Bloomington, Indiana, chapter, National Career Awards Chairman; and the members of the National Career Awards Competition Committee, Cam Cavanaugh of the New Jersey chapter, Cecelia Kline of the Arizona Valley-of-the-Sun chapter, Frances Dodson Rhome of the Indiana chapter, and Norma Williams of the Honolulu chapter.

With the publication of *The Luxury of Tears: The National Society of Arts and Letters Anthology of Short Stories,* the society has initiated the first in a realization of the achievements of the career award winners. It provides an enduring medium for the writer and the written word, the performer and the performance, the artist and the art.

Susan Park Schweiger
NATIONAL LITERATURE CHAIRMAN, 1988
NATIONAL SOCIETY OF ARTS AND LETTERS

14

LAURA   LEIGH   HANCOCK

The Dragon Lady and the Ponytail Plant

WHEN MRS. HAICHI is angry, as she was last night, she cooks mean. Handfuls of jalapeños fly into the curries and the sambal sauce froths with cayenne. Six gas jets roar and the cookpit fills with black-red smoke that would burn out a normal person's lungs. Walter leans into the sink and tries not to cough, and Mr. HaiChi flees to his office, where he steadies his hands over payroll and taxes, returning only when there's a call for his famous fried bananas and cream.

My eyes smart as I gaze through the order window, across the kitchen and down into the cookpit where Mrs. HaiChi waves her arms over four or five bubbling woks. I'd like to cross the forbidden kitchen and lead her out of the pit and away to some place cool and quiet, but the Dragon Lady never looks up. She just seasons and stir-fries with a vengeance that will eventually burn out her rage.

But not before it has penetrated the bamboo screens that separate the dark, narrow serving alley from the dining area.

Babies sense it first and howl through gummed saltines while first dates refold their napkins and bump knees under the sedate blue tablecloths. Even the plants, which are everywhere, in the windows, on the counters, hugging the walls, seem to crackle as I brush by, trying my best to ignore the thick-jawed patriarchs who raise their eyebrows and coat-sleeves and eventually succeed in flagging me down.

"Forty-five minutes! And not a sign of food!"

If the delay stretches to more than an hour, as it did last night, Mr. HaiChi creeps out of his office to fry up baskets of crisp papadams, which he sends out with me. Cool as yoghurt, I carry my pitcher among the tables as if it were a royal chalice, dousing frustrations and encouraging the customers to have pity on the poor cook who is single-handedly feeding over forty people. I treat them all like honored guests, filling every reasonable request and enduring their histrionics with a smile, for in my heart I'm serving only Mrs. HaiChi.

Last night the orders were appearing in the window almost ninety minutes late, and many were topped with a curled carrot, Walter's sly way of marking those dishes he knew to be fiendishly hot. He's the royal taster and I trust his judgment, delivering those curries with an extra pitcher of water, and a special smile. Then I rush back to the waitress station and dish up bowls and bowls of fresh coconut ice cream, the only thing that can truly extinguish the fire of the Dragon Lady's cooking.

Mrs. HaiChi's fury, which had lain dormant for weeks, exploded three times yesterday afternoon. First she caught the poultry deliverer knocking his ashes into the potted lemon tree. Then the linen man arrived with no napkins and a chef's coat two sizes too big. Finally the baker disregarded her order for separate boxes, and wrapped the jam thumbprints and almond tea cookies together in a fine jelly mess. Rolling up the sleeves on the starched white coat, Mrs. HaiChi cursed them all loudly and thoroughly, pausing only to wipe a bit of raspberry jam from the side of her mouth, and finger the jade lifesaver that hung on a gold chain around her neck.

16

I pity the recipient of Mrs. HaiChi's curses. The amulet is sorceror's jade, found by her grandmother long ago at the edge of the palace grounds, and it has not left Mrs. HaiChi's neck since the old woman died. And in the past year that I've worked at Asahla Khin I've seen the Dragon Lady's word become truth and her will reality, sending ill-favoured glassware crashing to the floor, and calling customers to the restaurant almost against their will.

"Where *is* our Fussy Old Man?" she'll ask, and if not that night, then the next I'll look up to hear his proper British clip asking for the table behind the screen.

Mrs. HaiChi has even worked her magic on me from time to time. The day we met, for instance—I was drinking coffee in a bakery just down the street from Asahla Khin, reading the want ads and trying to recover from the shock of my grandmother's death. The grand old lady had been the last of my family; shortly after her funeral I packed the old car she left me and drove west on the straightest road I could find.

The HaiChis were looking for someone to take the place of their Daughter Number Two, who had just left for medical school, and they liked the way I cleared my table when I was done, giving it a few quick sweeps and creasing the newspaper with the palm of my hand. As I passed their table, Mrs. HaiChi feigned confusion and held up her coffee cup for a refill. Exhausted to the point of despair, I nearly brushed by her outstretched hand, but something stopped me, and I found my lips curving into a smile as I took her cup and headed up to the counter. I even remembered to bring a fresh creamer to their table, and when I left Mr. HaiChi followed me out the door and offered me a waitressing job on the spot.

The work was harder than I imagined, the trays heavy and unmanageable, the food foreign and complex. Steam from the kitchen plastered my hair to my forehead, my feet ached, and I trembled each time Mrs. HaiChi yelled for a slice of lemon or a sprig of mint. One Saturday night at the height of the dinner rush, I found myself bent over the waitress sink, watching jasmine tea leaves swirl down the drain, thinking, I

17

can't go one more step. But again something outside myself pulled me up and back out onto the dining room floor, where I began to concentrate on the small things: uncorking a bottle, folding a napkin, placing a bowl of soup just so on the dark tablecloth.

Shortly after that night, Mr. HaiChi taught me how to balance the trays on my fingertips where they floated level and almost weightless. And Mrs. HaiChi began to feed me diluted curries, adding a little less water each night until my mouth came alive to the fire of her cooking. I learned to eat with my fingers and to carry dishes stacked all the way up to my elbows, and by the time June Rose arrived, I was not only a capable waitress, I was Daughter Number Three.

The HaiChis sponsored June Rose's immigration to America. A recent and wealthy widow, she assured her brother she would not be a burden: she had plans. Mr. and Mrs. HaiChi assumed that she had found an American boyfriend, and with Chinese discretion they inquired no further, merely signed the necessary papers and awaited her arrival. But the day June Rose walked into the restaurant it was clear she had intentions of a different sort.

I was gathering the lunch mats and setting the tables for dinner when the door jangled open and she clicked in, Mr. HaiChi a hound's length behind. A stunning woman, with richly swirled black hair and a face like a porcelain urn, June Rose swept by my greetings in a perfumed breeze and made her way to the front counter, pausing only to scratch at one of the tablecloths with a long, red nail. Taking a menu from the bamboo rack, she rapped on the side of the register.

"Ka-mee! I am here!"

Mrs. HaiChi wobbled out from the kitchen, wiping her grease-smeared glasses on her grease-smeared apron, then squinting through the whole blurry mess. The circle of jade hung dully at her neck and her brown-singed hair stuck out in every direction.

"June Rooose," she said, extending her arms across the counter, palms up so that the grease scars of the last eight years stood out dark and ugly against her pale skin. An angry

18

red blister laced her wrist.

"Ka-mee!" June Rose touched her fingertips lightly, then withdrew. Mr. HaiChi shifted from foot to foot in the background, and I began to snatch up placemats faster and faster.

"Ka-mee, there is so much to be done," she said, plucking idly at the Boston ivy that trailed across the counter. She had lived for years in her husband's native England, and spoke flawless Queen's English. "It lacks—ambience. People expect red tablecloths from a Chinese restaurant, and brass, and a Buddha by the door. But it can be done." June Rose opened the menu and sighed as she ran her finger down the price list. "Yes, I can do it. I can make a success of this place."

I froze behind the giant shiffalera, and only dimly heard the clatter of silverware on the floor. Kneeling, my eyes fixed on the two women, I groped for the fork and spoon and waited for the Dragon Lady's famous temper to blow June Rose out the door. But nothing happened, and after several moments passed I heard a small, unfamiliar voice say, "Thank you, June Rose, but we don't need your help."

As far as I know, the two women never spoke again, but the matter was far from settled. June Rose spun out the door with her brother on her heels, and Mrs. HaiChi motioned me over to the counter.

"What does that one know about the food business?" she demanded, eyes flashing like sapphires while her hands stroked and soothed the disturbed ivy. "What does she know about work? For thirty years she rode around on her husband's arm. No children, no struggle—what can she know about a business like ours?"

I flopped the placemats on the shelf above the register and went back to retrieve a few of the white paper napkins that had fallen out along the way.

"Do you know what this is?" Mrs. HaiChi asked when I returned to her side. She pointed to the eight darkly draped tables, the verdant baskets hanging from every possible support, the tasteful calligraphy on the walls. "This is my rice bowl, my only rice bowl. June Rose is very rich. Why must she steal from a poor beggar like me?"

I pulled a handful of forks from the plastic bin and examined the tines for stray grains of rice. "Maybe she's lonely," I said. "Maybe she wants to feel like she's needed."

"That one? Hah!" Mrs. HaiChi dropped the vine she was tending. "I'll tell you what she wants. She wants her brother to do her every command—and he will! But not me. I will die before I bow to that woman." Her face darkened and she grabbed my wrist with a desperation that scared me. "Come!"

Mrs. HaiChi pulled me through the waitress station, into the kitchen and right up to the edge of the cookpit. The smell of animal fat and oyster sauce hung thick in the air, and crusty black woks covered the grease-freckled walls. A rack of unlabelled jars and bottles stood in one corner.

"Do you know what that is?" she asked, squeezing my wrist.

I shook my head, my throat burning from the pepper in the air.

"That is hell," she said proudly. "*My* bloody hell."

From that day on, June Rose haunted Asahla Khin, coming two and three times a week to give her brother "business." At first she came alone, at any hour of the day, demanding to be served "whatever Ka-mee is fixing right now." But as time went on she acquired a string of escorts, wealthy Americans in sharp gray suits, who studied the menu longer than was necessary, and made notes over the wine list. If it wasn't too busy Mr. HaiChi joined them over a pot of tea, and smoke billowed from the cookpit.

"Investors," Mrs. HaiChi hissed. "She wants to own this place, to make me work for her. And that old fool"— she flipped a mass of fried rice-noodles with one deft turn, — "he'll do it. He'll sign the whole bloody business over to her in a minute."

"He wouldn't do that," I protested, leaning against the

refrigerator at the edge of the cookpit, the order in my hand forgotten. "Mr. HaiChi wouldn't do anything without asking you first."

"Hah!" Grease splattered triumphantly and flames shot up into the firehood. "Do you know what my husband did last week. He gave his dear sister a key to our house. *My* house. She has her own house. Why must she have mine too?"

"Did you tell him that it upset you?" I asked, handing her the order.

"What does that matter?" Mrs. HaiChi squinted over my writing and shook her head. "When Number One Sister says 'Jump!' he jumps. That is custom."

"Not here—" I began but Mrs. HaiChi waved me away.

"You must understand," she said. "I am American, but my husband is still very much Chinese."

Her words seemed to prove true overnight. Mr. HaiChi's shy good humor disappeared, and he shuffled nervously around the restaurant with hardly a joke or smile for anyone. When June Rose telephoned, as she did nearly every night, he shut the door to his office and spoke in low Chinese. At first I defended him, for I thought he only wished to spare his wife any mention of June Rose. But then the afternoon calls began, American voices I didn't recognize, who refused to speak to Mrs. HaiChi or leave a message if Mr. HaiChi wasn't there. And some days, when lunch was slow, I would stand at the counter and watch him sort the day's mail at the curbside box, pocketing one or two letters before bringing the routine circulars and bills into the restaurant. He went on long afternoon errands and returned empty-handed, raising bleak eyes when Mrs. HaiChi demanded the eggplant he had been sent to buy.

"My husband refuses to argue!" she exclaimed last week as the two of us sat in the kitchen making eggrolls. His passivity was, she implied with a flick of cabbage, a cardinal sin.

"How can he?" I asked indulgently. "It's not his nature."

"So, okay, in the little things." Mrs. HaiChi slapped a spoonful of filling on the wrapper, tucked the corners, and rolled it up. "But I'm talking a big thing, like cancer, like death. Carmen, he tells me nothing. Those phone calls, letters—nothing! Do you know what I found last week?"

I shook my head and concentrated on the thin flour skin before me. This was painstaking work, measuring out the cooked cabbage, folding the corners in to a point, painting the edges with cornstarch and rolling the whole thing up.

"There was a letter on the table at home," she said. "Opened. What was I supposed to do? Of course I read—and good thing! June Rose is scheming to bring the Old One, their mother, to America." Mrs. HaiChi zipped out another perfect eggroll. "Did we ever send for my mother? For any of my family? So why must I take care of his family now?"

My product looked like a lumpy rolled carpet next to Mrs. HaiChi's neat little bundles. She laid her hand on mine to prevent me from taking another wrapper. "If that Old One dies here, the body must be shipped home. Do you know how expensive it is to ship a body? Take the money, I tell him, take it and go see her while she is alive. It is foolish to spend it on a body. But oh, he is angry. He doesn't like to hear that word. Body!"

I didn't like it either; it sounded like a curse on the Dragon Lady's lips. I climbed down from my stool and went into the cookpit to start the flame under the oil.

"That word doesn't bother me!" Mrs. HaiChi called. "My mother, what is she now? A body! My sister? A body! So alive and young—all bodies now!"

It took me four tries to light the burner, and I waited by the stove for the oil to bead and bubble. When it was hot enough to bounce a drop of water, I went back to the kitchen and collected several eggrolls. Mrs. HaiChi still worked behind a pyramid of dough and cabbage.

"I'm not afraid of that word," she said. "I would rather be a body than live like this, vultures picking at my rice bowl."

The oil churned and hissed when I lowered the eggrolls in the fry basket, and the hot spit stung my hands but I didn't jerk away. I thought its bite would help me understand the slit-eyed woman who had come to stand by my elbow, a dozen eggrolls cradled against her small, fierce chest.

Mrs. HaiChi was spritzing her jungle when I arrived at Asahla Khin yesterday afternoon and she motioned me in the side door which had been left open for the floor cleaners who came every Friday. I joined her at the front ledge, where she was pinching and petting a garden of miniature tropicals, dwarfed by years of root-binding and dehydration. They were her prized collection, a microcosm of the country she had left eight years before, and she tamped the soil around each one carefully, her mouth working. At length she extracted a spray of leaves from all the others and held it out for me to see.

"Look, Carmen," she said. "How can the little ponytail know it's spring behind all this glass?"

The phone began to ring and Mrs. HaiChi motioned me away. "You answer," she said. "Mr. HaiChi is gone to the warehouse."

"Let me speak to my brother," June Rose snapped when she heard my voice.

When I replied that Mr. HaiChi was out on an errand, she made a disbelieving sound, and left terse instructions for a party of two at seven o'clock. Mrs. HaiChi limped past me as I was hanging up.

"It was That One, wasn't it?" she asked, her face darkening when I nodded. "Why must she torture my last days? Carmen! I am one step from the grave. One step! Why can't this last step be easy?"

The phone rang again—a party of four at six-thirty—and then almost immediately a call for three people at eight. By the time I finished making the reservations and could return to the kitchen, Mrs. HaiChi was up to her elbows in deboned chicken. She motioned me toward a vat of beef curry, and I went to work measuring eight-ounce servings into small plastic containers. "Who comes with?" she asked, after a few minutes of silence.

"Mr. Task," I said, my eyes never leaving the scales in front of me. Mr. Task was a lawyer; I had seen his card on the bulletin board by the front register.

"Oh, they are up to something," Mrs. HaiChi said, and her voice sounded so small and alone that I longed to go over to her, and put my arms around her. But she was all elbows and chicken fat, her knife flashing dangerously in and out of breasts and drumsticks. So I stayed where I was, dumbly dishing beef and gravy.

"The worst is not June Rose," Mrs. HaiChi said finally, laying her knife aside. "The worst is me, Carmen, the horrible old woman I've become. Old friends wouldn't recognize me. My own mother would say, 'Where is Ka-mee? Where is my sweet, generous daughter?'"

Her small, hooded eyes were almost invisible, and tears hung on her lashes. "When I was young, someone would admire my belt. 'Take! Take!' I'd say. There were more. More belts, more parties, more friends. But now—" She drew her sleeve across her face. "Now I am frightened of another old woman."

Mrs. HaiChi shook the tears from her cheeks and motioned me out of the kitchen. "Go flip the sign, Carmen," she said. "It's time to work."

There were already two parties waiting when I unlocked the door, and Mr. HaiChi was pulling into the parking lot. I was so busy seating them and taking pots of hot jasmine tea to their tables that I didn't see him come in, but when I took the orders back to the kitchen he was already standing at the sink shelling shrimp, his hands ripping deftly through the thin, pungent husks. Neither cook nor waitress nor dishwasher, he could do all three, helping out whenever he was needed, at the sink or register or fry-pot. In the old days he was always laughing and joking, his shy smile soothing even the most irate customer. But last night he hardly responded to my greeting, and I noticed he and Mrs. HaiChi weren't speaking at all. When I told him that Mr. Lamb, one of our most faithful customers, had just arrived, he looked relieved at the excuse to leave the kitchen. After he had gone, Mrs. HaiChi called me over to the cookpit.

"I was right," she whispered. "Mr. Task is bringing the papers to sign, to make June Rose part-owner."

"How do you know?" I asked, my heart as cold as the bag of ice I had taken from the freezer.

"That old fool told me," Mrs. HaiChi said. She ladled a shallow puddle of oil into the wok and lit the burner. "He said, 'Ka-mee, I think it is a good idea. If anything ever happens to me, you will have June Rose.' Hah! Like a stone around my neck. Like a rock in my shoe."

She dished a spoonful of garlic into the oil where it sizzled lightly. "I told him no."

I grinned and took the ice to the sink, where I shook half over the curled pink shrimp. Good-bye June Rose! The garlic smell, as I returned to the edge of the cookpit, made it hard for me to smile as large as I wanted to. "What did he say?" I asked.

Mrs. HaiChi shrugged, and the mammoth chef's coat sagged off her shoulders. "He thinks I am mean and hard. He says I am not the girl he married. But still I refuse. If June Rose comes, I go. My recipes go. My spices go. Without me, this shop is nothing."

The door jangled and I hurried out to seat several parties, one right after the other, my feet hardly touching the floor as I ran back and forth, filling drink orders and delivering appetizers. People could fill the whole restaurant and line up outside the door and I wouldn't despair. June Rose was soon to be vanquished! I could hardly wait to see the angry red scrawl of her lipstick when Mr. HaiChi delivered the final verdict.

The seven o'clock rush had just hit when she and Mr. Task arrived, and I dropped everything I was doing and rushed to meet them at the door, determined to keep June Rose out of the kitchen. I led them to the two-top behind the front ledge, where they could neither see nor be seen by anyone in the back. June Rose scowled when I brought their water.

"Have you ordered Singapore tea as I suggested?" she asked. "No? Two coffees, then, and whatever Ka-mee would like to cook for us."

Back in the kitchen Mrs. HaiChi slung several sticks of satay onto the grill. "If I cook what I want, June Rose will eat shit," she muttered, thrusting a plate of cold shumai into my hands. "Take this to keep that one in her seat."

June Rose was running her long nails through the plant on their table when I returned with the coffee and shumai, and she didn't bother to lean back. I arranged the dishes around her silk-wrapped arms, smiling determinedly at Mr. Task, who beamed at the plate of food. When I returned a few minutes later to replace the empty dishes with fried rice and satay in peanut sauce, June Rose demanded to see her brother.

"Mr. HaiChi is very busy helping his wife," I said sweetly, "but I'm sure he'll come to see you the first chance he gets."

Just then a party of nine arrived and I forgot all about June Rose in the rush of pulling tables together and handing out menus all around. Like all large parties, they had a set routine of questions and special requests. Which wine is drier, bolder, heavier? Do you use MSG? May I have butter on my chapati? My husband would like double hot mustard, and I want none at all. Can you leave the onions off my salad? I'm allergic to anything that grows underground.

The food was coming out very slowly, every other dish marked with a carrot, and I could hear Walter coughing at the sink, but the thought of June Rose's defeat kept my spirits high. As I was removing the soup bowls from my large table I saw Mr. HaiChi disappear behind the front ledge with a fresh pot of coffee and two boats of coconut ice cream. I longed to peek through the thick jungle at June Rose's face, but there were too many customers plucking at my sleeves, and miming the final stages of starvation.

I was waiting for a side order of chutney when Mr. HaiChi returned to the waitress station, set the empty coffee pot on the counter and went into his office without a word. A moment later Mr. Task came up to the counter and asked for a toothpick; he looked well-fed and angry. Behind him I saw

June Rose whirl out the front door like a small tropical storm. When Walter put the bowl of chutney on the tray I slid the whole thing onto my shoulder as if it weighed nothing at all. June Rose had been ousted! The restaurant was saved!

When ten o'clock came I flipped the sign and went into the kitchen to tell Mrs. HaiChi that the evening was over. She had just finished with the last fried rice, and she leaned heavily on my arm as I helped her out of the cookpit. "Everything's back to normal," I whispered.

She shook her head at me and leaned against the freezer. "You can't understand," she said, looking a little dazed. "How can I ever trust him, Carmen? How do I know June Rose won't be back with some new scheme, tomorrow or the day after?"

Mrs. HaiChi handed me her glasses to wipe, then shuffled off to the office where her husband had been doing payroll ever since June Rose left. Her voice made me sad, but I didn't believe her. There was no reason we couldn't go back to the old days when we were a family, the days before June Rose. Mr. HaiChi would convince her. This thought cheered me, and I went back out onto the floor to finish clearing the dishes.

I saved June Rose's table for last, neither surprised nor dismayed over the meager tip tucked under the ice cream boat. Balancing my tray on the front ledge I swept everything off the table and had just begun to fold in the edges of the tablecloth when I sensed that something was terribly wrong. Straightening slowly, my hand tight on the tray, I gazed around the little corner. Something was horribly off-balance, impossibly out of line.

The ponytail plant was gone. I felt it before I actually saw the ring of dirt where the clay pot had been. I searched through the plants on the ledge, under the table and in the corner, but I couldn't find it anywhere. Leaving the cream-crusted dishes on the tray, I finally dragged myself to the office door. Mr. HaiChi called me in.

"All done, Carmen?" he asked absently. "The checks will be ready in a minute."

"Someone stole the ponytail plant," I blurted.

Mrs. HaiChi was fingering a grease burn on her forearm and she looked up sharply, two red circles glowing high on her flat cheeks. Tears oozed instantly from the corners of her puffy eyes.

"Who?" she asked.

I could see those bright nails combing through the dwarfed leaves, but I didn't think the tiny office could hold my accusation. "I don't know," I mumbled.

"Bastards!" Mrs. HaiChi struggled to the edge of the lounge chair. "They come, they eat, they go. Do they say 'Thank you'? Do they say they had a wonderful time? No. They eat and they drink, they ask for my recipes and now they steal my soul. Why, I ask you. Why?"

Mr. HaiChi's back stiffened but he never paused. His pen glided over the paychecks and he leaned ever so slightly away from his wife's rage.

Mrs. HaiChi tugged at her already unbuttoned collar and flushed a deep rose. "Six years I tended that plant," she said. "Six years I water it, and bind its roots. Now I curse the one who stole it. May he have six bad years. May he fall sick and gasping. May he hurt like I hurt, and may his family—"

"Ka-mee!" Mr. HaiChi roared, his chair screeching across the floor. He threw his pen down and it rolled off the desk. "Enough!"

I had never heard him raise his voice, or do anything in anger, and I drew back in the doorway. Mrs. HaiChi recoiled too, but only for a second. Then her surprise turned to cunning and she nodded, tight-lipped, as if another one of her prophesies had come true. She didn't flinch when her husband leaned over his chair back and thrust two whitened fists into her face.

"If someone offered you two hands, Ka-mee," he said, in a voice so bitter and cruel that I hardly recognized it, or the face twisting behind the words, "two hands, compassion or power—which would you choose?"

"I'd choose curses," Mrs. HaiChi said sweetly, pulling on the jade around her neck. "Curses on the brothers of thieves."

There was not a sound in the restaurant last night as we waited, the three of us, for Mrs. HaiChi's words to come true.

CAROL VIVIAN SPAULDING

Not If, When

WE DON'T LIKE to speak about the other one because we think it will make all the difference. Mama has said as much herself. She says, "Get away from me. When I lose it you can treat me like a baby." Nobody wants to treat her like that, but it is hard not to with a woman in her condition. Today Mama sits in her printed shift, her thin, bloodless leg resting down to the chrome footplate. Tomorrow she could have two stumps bulging from her lap and nothing left to fill her pink puff slipper. May says Mama's good leg's not going anywhere without her, but we know better. This from Dr. Wickson: it's not if, it's when.

May and I live in the apartment under Mama. Mornings I go upstairs and shake her shoulder. I ask her does she have to pee. "Get away from me," she says and hoists herself into her chair, wheels into the toilet, locks the door. Yesterday she fell. I might as well have had no legs at all, no arms or head either for all the good I could do standing there listening to her try to pick herself up off the linoleum. I was so steamed I told her, "Now pick yourself up." But this morning I'm worried about adverse effects.

I set out her bottle of Lucky and a fresh pack of Nows on the card table. In the kitchen I put her egg on to boil and start some toast. I have to leave the food in the oven so that maybe she'll eat it when I'm out of the way. I hear her wheel out, turn on the tube and start switching channels. She finds a show, twists the cap off her beer, flicks her Bic. Maybe she'll eat, maybe she won't. I'm not up to combat this morning. She won't let me get her a remote control. She won't let me feed her cats or scrub her sink. "Find a man to fuss over," she'll tell me. "I've still got one good leg."

I call to her through the kitchen divider. "You feeling all right this morning?"

"I'm fine, baby."

"Shall we go ahead and keep our appointment with Dr. Wickson?" I venture.

Silence. May's the only one who can get her to go. She lies to her: "He's just gonna look at it and take some pictures."

"You remember Ila, the receptionist, Mama? She says she'll have to charge us if we miss again."

Mama lived too hard. There were two who never even made an appearance because she left the state and found a sort of doctor, blew her savings twice. Said she bled for a week both times—"Could have done it better myself with a garden tool." May and I suspect we have different fathers. Mother flew a little, between wars. There were pilots, sailors, corporate executives. She lived in Alaska. Drove a cab. Pressed nuts and bolts during the war. She said she could drink Daddy right under the table. Now she perches in that chair, a stick of a woman with a few tufts of hair and eyes huge and amazed behind thick lenses. Sometimes they water up at May. "Don't smoke, Pearl. Look at me now," and she lifts the leg a little, works the toes like she wants to make sure she can still operate them.

After a while, Mama gets bored with the tube and lowers the sound. "Sue, bring me my crewel kit," she hollers. So I shut the faucet, dry my hands, go to her room where I see she hasn't made the bed she wouldn't let me make, and get out

31

the kit from her dresser. This month it's a harbor view: pier and gulls with drifting boat.

"1939, dammit, '39!" she shouts to the game show contestant. I set her net and yarn and needle on the cardtable. "Mama," I start.

"Stay, fool! Stay!" she shouts. The contestant holds at one thousand. I turn the sound all the way down. She waves an arm at me. "Get away from there, Sue."

"You'll forget your cigarette again, doing two things at once," I warn. Sometimes she takes one puff, then she leaves a snake of ash that winds up on the carpet.

Mama snuffs out the cigarette. "Do I look like I'm straining myself, baby?"

I snicker. "You're so hard. You think I haven't got better things to do?"

Mama hunches forward in that way she has and peers our over her rims. "Baby, go on and give me some peace. Haven't you got a life?"

Her cats—they are all filthy flea-ridden strays—brush up against her leg or through the bottom of her chair. Who will feed them? I think of how it's just another chore, to know what I know, though maybe it will be easier when it's done with. I think of how when you have no legs at all, someone has to come and turn you in the night.

"All right," I tell her. "All right, fine. I've got to go down and get your hair rinse anyway. But don't forget—Dr. Wickson this afternoon."

"Sue," she says to me when I'm halfway out the door.

I stop and sigh and turn.

"Run and get my lipstick before you go."

What with always worrying about the leg and me like I was the only daughter she had to care for her anymore, Mama's got to punish me when it's her mistakes she's paying for.

Downstairs is so quiet with May gone. When I walk into our place I feel like I hardly live there. How can I keep up Mama's place and my own too? May's got her brochures and applications scattered everywhere. She's had this idea to go to travel school so she can host ten-day tours of the Orient, but she's been studying over the literature for a year now and she still works at the Costco.

Since I have the day off, Mama can wait. I do the breakfast dishes, the two glasses, two plates, two of everything. I fold the outfits May draped over the sofa, the ones she tried out for work today, though I don't know why she can't make up her mind since she has to wear a smock. I run the sweeper, water my plants, and stick the jockey shorts and tee-shirt in the hamper with our clothes.

Then I have to search May's room to find the hair rinse she brought home. She said she couldn't find Mama's usual color, and I see she'll have to settle for Autumn Mist. Mama's hair is fried from the chemicals. I don't see the good in beautifying herself at this point, but May says I'm just trying to make Mama feel old, so I go along with it, though it turns out May hasn't got time to rinse Mama's hair or hardly say hello since Alex.

It's strange the way a place can have the feel of a person when he's not even in it. What is it? A man's smell, maybe. The wrinkles in May's sheets. I ought to know Alex pretty well since he practically lives here. He builds cabinets during the day and usually rides his motorbike here at night, where he fixes the oven or unclogs the drain, eats our food, watches our TV and goes to bed with little May. He's making her a hope chest. I take this as a sign of his intentions. I think he'll work out okay, though lately they do more fighting than they do loving. "Outta my face, slimebag," she'll say. May's got a mouth that doesn't need to shout. Poor Alex. He scares easily for such a big person.

When I get back upstairs, it's already time for lunch. Mama's fallen asleep in her chair, the tube on, her head thrown back, mouth open. When she stretches out like that you can almost tell how she used to be if you look hard enough. She had long, elegant legs. Gorgeous gams. Whenever she sat, she would stretch them out in front out of her, crossing them at the ankles to give the best view. She had the sheerest hose, the highest heels. May and I used to wobble around in them for practice when we were kids, trying to walk like she told us, setting one foot before the other in a line, instead of side by side.

I scoot right past Mama and get out some pressed turkey. Then May breezes in, tiptoes to the kitchen and sets down the case of Lucky and the carton of Nows—a week's supply—on the table. I put a finger to my lips to tell her to shush before she opens her mouth. "She's gonna cross me, I know it."

"She told you no?" May asks. Before I can answer she pulls a Costco pineapple cake from her sack. "Look at dessert."

"Better work your magic," I tell her, and she follows me out to Mama, who, with her head still thrown back, tells us, "Leave me alone." Her eyes come open; she grips the arms of her chair and pulls herself upright.

"Mama," May begins. "Dr. Wickson just wants to have a look at it. He maybe wants to brag on you for how well you've held up so far."

Mama reaches for May's hand and squeezes. May says, "Or howabout this. Howabout we play a game of dominoes and eat some lunch? Then we'll watch Jeopardy and after that we'll go see Dr. Wickson."

"Don't baby me, Pearl. It brings me down, and you know how Sue's fussing tires me."

"Oh, that's just Sue. I won't baby you, Mama. It's just that I won't see you tonight. Alex is coming over."

"Atta girl," she says.

So we eat turkey sandwiches and then slice the cake. May takes a beer, then another. I take one myself.

"Howabout that beau of yours," Mama says. She's not eating a thing and lights another cigarette. "He's a handsome dog."

May snickers. "Weak mind, strong back, what can I say?"

"He's not stupid," I say.

34

"Are you kidding? I ask him what's the capital of Italy. He doesn't know. So I say, okay what about the U.S.? He says, Los Angeles, no, New York. Get a clue, bucko, I say to him, and he just stares at me, like he thinks I speak Tunisian."

Mama's looking from one of us to the other with her big eyes, like everything is new to her. "What did you ask him that for?" she says.

May fixes her collar for her, gives her a peck. "We about ready to go?"

It's the same as ever at Dr. Wickson's. Mama shoos me out of the exam room because she can't even let me help her into her gown. And it's always then, when May and I are waiting, that I picture her, the collar bone jutting out to the thin shoulders, the breasts fallen to the belly where the skin is stacked in folds. The stump, pink and smooth, like the leg had been coaxed off gently, without pain. I can never figure out how this is so clear to me, since I've seen it once—maybe once. But it makes me think of the endless stretch of days ahead, when Mama won't hardly be able to move at all without me. Sometimes it's like the good leg's already gone, and there's two stumps alike, pink and smooth, like babies' heads. I sit quietly thinking these thoughts while May is up chatting with Ila.

"She's strong as a horse," May says today. "You should see her lift herself up outta that chair. I suppose most people wouldn't take it that way. Most people would give up and let others do for them. But as long as you've got a leg to stand on . . ." and I tune out. She knows. She knows as well as I do but she never lets on.

It's the same as always. Blood pressure, okay. Circulation, sluggish but stable. Mama says she likes the part where he massages her leg. She says if he'd do that every day she wouldn't have the phantom pains, but he's the only one who can do it right.

Then Dr. Wickson comes out and gives me the look. He and I have this understanding. The look says, any day now—

could be without warning. But May and Dr. Wickson don't communicate very well, so when she insists Mama's doing fine, he has to shrug and say, "Wait and see."

May sort of cuzzies up to him, leaning into her hip and tilting her head up. He's very tall. "You just want her to have no legs because you like the thought of helpless women, don't you?"

Poor Dr. Wickson looks to me, then back to May. "It's been my experience that for people in your mother's condition, it's only a matter of time." Course he could put it another way. He doesn't have to make it sound like she's going to die.

May eyes the doctor like she's only just now figured him out. "Get real," she says.

Thank God Ila wheels Mama out. We all look. The leg is shiny and has some color to it. Mama's applied fresh lipstick and rearranged her hair.

Ila's very chatty today. "I'll get that address for you, Mrs. Neuman. They have a whole catalogue of kits. The pear tree I'm talking about takes over a month, but then you can hang it on the wall."

I go behind the chair and try to take the handles, but Mama slaps at my hands and then wheels forward before I get a grip. "Get away from me for once," she spits out. Lord. Ila titters like she thinks it's cute. "My, my," I say, "my, my."

May pulls me towards the door and says through her teeth, "Sue, people don't say my my my my."

"See you soon, Mrs. Neuman," Ila says, back in position at her desk. Dr. Wickson has disappeared.

"My, my," I say to Mama. "Aren't we cranky today?"

"I'd like to see her get through the day," I tell May that evening. "Without me." I'm in the tub trying to soak up a little peace of mind.

May's got her head tilted back; she's squirting Charley on. She pulls her top out, squirts, lifts her hair, squirts, rubs her wrists together. "Sue, she's just now at her best the days she sees Dr. Wickson." She pokes around her jewelry box for earrings. "I'll tell you what else. She could live to a hundred-and-one no matter what you do."

"You're so hard," I say. "Why can't you stand by me? That leg's got to go and it's not gonna be any easier if you pretend otherwise."

She bends at the waist, shoots up, whips her hair around her shoulders. She peers into the vanity, makes a face. "Don't tell me—it's not if, it's when."

I scoot down in the tub and slip my shoulders under the water. May's in such a hurry she shuts the bathroom light without thinking and closes the door. Before I can open my mouth to holler, I decide I like it that way. Warm in the water, dark and quiet. My legs make slipping sounds in the bubbles. My arms are smooth. I'm so still I can hear the bubbles whispering as they give, each tiny breath of bubble along my stomach and knees and chest. I listen for his motorbike until the water gets cool and May opens the front door to Alex and I hear them for only a moment and they leave. Then the dark is no longer peaceful but grows thick like I have to wade my way to the light switch. I shiver, dry myself, and instead of getting dressed and going up to help Mama into bed, I pull on my bathrobe, I'm so tired suddenly, and lie on top of the bed.

I awake once, startled; I think it is when the TV goes off upstairs. For a few moments my heart pounds with guilt, with anger. But after a while, the need to sleep settles into me, and for once it feels delicious and forgetful and luxurious not to be needed.

When I awake again, I hear May giggling and stumbling in the front room. I cannot hear Alex, but I can always feel when he's in the house, a feeling that I ought to stand up straighter and pull my belly in. Tonight it takes them no time at all to get down to business. May's giggles become whimpers and then low moans like an unabashed cow and never a peep out of Alex, even when that bed starts rocking and those springs start going eee-er, eee-er, eee-er. But tonight he does say something, loud and clear. It comes as a shock to me he can speak at all, and he says to May, like he knew I could hear, like even Mama could hear from upstairs where she lies, her chair right up against the bed, like it was not simply a command for my sister, pale and sweet beneath him, but one for all concerned. Loud and clear, he tells her, "Turn over."

So May can't get her fill of Alex and I get a mother with one good leg. Sometimes I feel the injustice of it, and I want to slap myself for refusing Lyle enough times to where he takes Trinnie out after work when it might have been me. There's boys enough have been in my pants. One, anyway. I say things like that just to see how they sound. That's not what I call it at all.

In the morning I hear them again before I even open my eyes. I think it's a form of abuse the way two people can carry on in a nearby room when there's others wanting peace. May's whooping it up in there. They must be about out of the K-Y jelly she keeps near her bed.

I lie still, my eyes closed, because when I open them I see the daylight straining at the curtains. Then I always feel compelled to get up, and when I get up I usually stay up, and pretty soon I've brushed my teeth, dressed, and am on my way upstairs. So I lie still. My sheets are cool. They're cooler against my bare skin. They're cool underneath me. My pillows are cool, one against my chest, the other, cool, underneath me. I think of how still the rest of me is, and of Alex with his skin where the pillows are, not white and soft and cool, but brown and hard and cool, then not cool, then not just my hands moving, neither of us cool, not cool at all. My eyes are still closed. Then they are still closed, still closed, still closed.

But I can't keep them closed because I hear May. The titter of her feet and her chatter moving around the room. Where did I drop my kimono? she is thinking. I hear Alex say something, low, but when the door opens it's only May's chatter, amplified. She's clattering in the kitchen, cracking eggs. I don't want to move, but my bathrobe is waiting on its hook and Mama needs to be waked soon.

Two raps on my door. "Yoo-hoo, Sue!" she sings. "Whyn't you get up now? We have a guest." I can't make out why all the fuss since it's only Alex; at least, it's only Alex to her. But when I'm done in the bathroom and I go out, my hair swept up in a twist and pinned with May's pearl barrette, I see there's no Alex straddling a chair in the breakfast nook, sipping his mug of coffee. It hits me.

"Sue, meet Wayne," she says to me.

I'm there long enough to gather that he's a three-piecer with almost no hair, before I walk right past them and head upstairs. She can straddle him like Debra Winger in "An Officer and a Gentleman" for all I care, but Mama's waiting. Poor Alex. Poor poor poor poor Alex.

Mama's already watching her show, and she's fixed herself toast and got out a beer. She's hunched over her project in the circle of light from the lamp, making little tugs at the yarn with the big needle. Even her cats are fed. I realize I cannot remember what color Mother's hair used to be. Was it my auburn? May's strawberry blond? Maybe it was jet black and I have simply forgotten how she could have ever been young. Anyway, today it will be Autumn Mist whether that suits her or not.

I'm fuming about May, and there's only one thing I can think of to do—to take the best care of Mama I can, for better or for worse, for as long as Mama has. She looks up at me after a while, her eyes huge behind those lenses.

"Morning, Mama. Did you pee already?"

"Baby," she says to me. She yanks at a stitch, stabs the needle back.

"What is it?"

"Say good morning, goddam you."

Our eyes lock, and Mama chuckles because I don't have a comeback. I let that one slide, merely heading for the kitchen to wash and rinse her few dishes and then to fix a jello salad. I hear the little gasp from the bottle when she twists off the cap. Saturday Classics is on, though I can't make out what picture it is. I stir some ice cubes in the jello and set it in the fridge. Then I start chopping the celery. I can hear voices from the TV but I can't make out the words, only background music, murmured conversation between a man and a woman. I'm chopping with a vengeance, and I'm think-ing one day soon it'll be just me and Mama and only two legs between the both of us and both of those mine. It's like they're not my hands chopping. . . . I could lose a fingertip if I don't find a way to calm down. "Wait and see," Dr. Wickson tells us, "wait and see." I make a rhythm in my head to the words as I'm chopping. Pretty soon, I'm on my fourth stalk, slicing off the pale, flowery part at the top, when I hear from the front room. "Oooh!" Then, "Sue, oh!"

"Is it your phantom pains again?" I call to Mama.

"Get in here," she tells me. "I'm dying."

I rush out, rush back and set down the knife, rush back out. She's doubled up over her one good leg.

"Where does it hurt?" I say. "Oh my God," I say.

"My leg," she says through her teeth. I see the top of her head, the pink scalp through her tufts of hair.

"Which one, Mama? The one that's there or the one that isn't there?"

"Get May, then," she tells me. "I don't have time for it, Sue."

But I'm still standing there, because what has it all been for if I can't be there now? I kneel on the floor and hold her. "Tell me what it is," I say. She's so taut and small in my arms. Her leg is turned awkwardly on the footplate, as though it was not part of her, just there between us. And I see I expected it to be different somehow, that there ought to be more ceremony attached to losing a limb, that I don't, not really, want it to start just now. We are still together, my arms around her for a long while, until I hear her breathe and relax into me, her head resting in the crook of my neck. Dead weight. Mama, don't let it happen now. We are still, together. After a while, she says to me, "They're getting worse."

"Why didn't you tell me?"

"They're mostly at night."

"How could you not tell me? What did Dr. Wickson say?"

"It's what I said to him."

"Which was what, Mama?"

"I said to get away from me. It's my leg."

I could wheel the woman right into the closet.

She works the toes again. "It's my leg to lose in my own good time."

So what is there to do but ease her back in her chair, take that chair and wheel her to her room, help her into bed, get her medicine. She won't let me take her glasses off, and she fixes me with those eyes. "Why do you think I'm going to die?"

I pull the sheets up over her. "Mama, I think I'll have a cigarette. Will you rest?"

She nods and takes my hand. "Give me peace. You girls. All right?" But she doesn't know May's downstairs with this Wayne character.

"All right, fine," I tell her. Maybe I'll tell her what May's up to. "Rest now," I say.

I sit down with a cigarette in the chair next to Mama's bed and think on what to do about May. I can't call her any names she hasn't already been called. I can't tell Mama what she's up to because what would Mama care? May will wear out this Wayne character. In a few months he'll be nothing to anybody around here except the one who came between Alex and the man she has yet to move on to.

Mama hasn't said a word about my hair or the pearl barrette; usually she notices when I wear May's things. My hair's not so long, but I slide the barrette out, fluff my hair and arrange it around my shoulders. I throw my head back, take a long, slow drag and gaze out the window down to the street. Mama's quiet. Maybe she'll sleep all day. I prop my feet up on the end table, thinking of what my life would be like if things happened to me. Sometimes, when I dream the leg is gone, I keep waking from my dream to turn her. Every two hours, all night long, I wake thinking it's time to turn her. If I left her even one night, with her skin so old and tired,

Mama would wake with bedsores.

So I'll turn her over, then I'll maybe sit and smoke near the window. On summer nights I'll lean out and let my hair fall across my face and my bare shoulders will shine in the moonlight. I'll be still, so I can listen for the motorbike, and when Mama snores I'll turn her again.

I have a good view of the street. I'll see the glint of the chrome as he cruises past. At the corner, he'll circle and cruise past again. Then he'll chug into the driveway, shut off the ignition and sit there straddling his machine. He'll look up with his mooning face. "Do you want to go for a ride?"

Maybe I do. "You're drunk," I'll say.

"Had some beer. Want to come out?"

Maybe I do. But I will have to give it serious consideration. What will I ever do with Mama when Alex wants to go for a ride? If I to stay where I am, Mama will sleep through the night without a peep. If I go, it will be the very night she needs me. She'll have an attack and I'll be flying down the streets, my arms around his middle, my chest against his back, my hair whipping in the windy night.

To have something on May, what pleasure. I'll take my time telling her the news. "Remember Alex?" I'll say.

"What about Alex?"

"Nothing. He hasn't forgotten about you."

She'll throw her head back and work her shoulders like she's got a twitch way deep inside her. "I'm unforgettable." Then she'll seem to think about this and it will bust her up. "What, is he mooning around for me? Is he on the prowl?"

"I saw him last night—again. He says he gets lonely after work and has a few beers. He asked me would I like to go with him."

"What'd you say?"

"I told him I wouldn't."

"Too bad for both of you."

"Maybe so. He asked would I like to just go for a ride."

"And what'd you say then?"

"I said 'Shh, you'll wake Mama.' "

"And you went?"

"Maybe so."

I guess she won't be too shaken up about it. Why should I care? She can tramp in and out with any man she wants to. She can tramp off to China. I'll be here. I'll slide the window open. "Shh," I'll say.

He'll insist. "Come out for a ride with me."

I'll shrug and remind him gently. "Mama."

She'll be resting quietly. Even while sleeping, she'll try to turn herself over, clench her fists at her side as though her arms could take the place of her lost legs. Her cheek may be pressed into the pillow so that it's hard for her to lift her head. She'll want to breathe freely, to be on her back, even after I've just turned her. I can't always be turning her. Not if, but when Alex comes, I may have to leave her that way for a while. It isn't safe. I've heard of accidents—suffocations—because people have had no one to turn them in the night. I'll have to bear that in mind. For now there's peace here, and cricket song to remind me that the nights are getting warmer. Dr. Wickson says it is only a matter of time. There's Mama beside me, no pain. There's May maybe going off to China. And the chug of a motorbike, Alex calling me to the window. Mama will be quiet then. No more pain. I'll go to the window, lean out. "Shh," I'll say.

DAVID ANTHONY DOBBS

Placing Protection

"Douglas," said Emily. "It's getting dark."

Already on his knees, Doug bent closer over the mushroom he was trying to photograph.

"Go on," he told her. "I'll catch up."

He looked up long enough to see her walk away, then turned and got down on his elbows to steady the camera. The light was fading quickly. Already the exposure reading had changed from what it was before Emily had interrupted him. He focused, took two exposures, moved, refocused, took two more. As the light faded the mushroom's cap, pale lilac with a sulfurous-looking aureole, seemed increasingly luminous against the darkening soil from which it grew. Excited, he took six more exposures, then changed lenses and took four more, and then the light on the forest floor was too dim. He shouldered his pack and set off to catch up with Emily.

She waited at the forest's edge. Tiny white blossoms grew in the grass at her feet. She picked one, snapping its fine stalk, and held it in her palm. The flower rolled across her hand, hard as an artichoke heart, and fell to the earth.

Before her the trail rose through broad meadows, following the valley north and then east around the shoulder of a long, double-peaked mountain on the right. The whole valley lay in deepening shadow. She wondered how long they would have to walk in the dark.

Doug dropped his pack near Emily's, sat on it, and opened his water bottle.

"It's pretty," he said.

"You should see it in the light."

He looked at her, tapped her pack with his foot.

"You haven't been here that long."

"Long enough." She flicked away the piece of grass she had been fiddling with and looked at him. "You rushed me all afternoon to get out here, Doug, and then we get up here and you make me wait. . . ."

"And that makes you angry."

"You know it does. Especially when it gets dark and we're not where we want to be. We aren't, are we?"

He took a drink from the water bottle. "We have a mile and a half left," he said, "but the moon comes up in half an hour. A big fat one. It's a clear night. We can walk by that."

"You're—you knew all this before? About the moon?"

"Yeah. I mean, I saw it last night."

She looked at him and shook her head. "Well, I didn't know that, Doug. I didn't know the big fat moon was coming up."

"I guess I should have told you or something."

"Yes, or something," she said. But what, neither of them seemed to know.

Emily lay in her bag dreaming. She dreamt she was camping in Yosemite with her brother, as she used to do ten years before. Waking, she thought for a moment that she was there, that Allen was outside meditating in the early sun. Then she sat up and remembered where she was. She was in the Swiss Alps, not Yosemite, and it was Doug, not Allen she was with. Allen was in business school in the United States.

She pulled her sleeping bag closer around her shoulders. Doug's lay empty beside her. Usually they slept with them zipped together, but last night the zippers didn't seem to want to mate, and Doug's flashlight kept flickering out, until finally, cold and exasperated and not feeling particularly amorous anyway, they had lain them out separately. It was, she realized as she lay there slowly waking, the first time they'd slept in separate bags, and while she had missed being curled against Doug's warmth in the night she had to admit that it had its advantages, such as not being woken when he got up early. He was always getting up early to do something—to fish, to shoot some pictures, to do some early bouldering, or to take a walk "when the light was good," as he said. Only occasionally did he stay in bed, either here or at home, and sleep late as she liked to do. The first time they had slept together, though—in a place much like this, in fact, a high meadow surrounded by peaks—he stayed with her then, and (my God, she thinks, remembering) they made love right there in those noisy sleeping bags with their friends not ten feet away outside making breakfast, their boots clunking softly against the frozen ground. Surely they had heard them doing it. She had moved toward him as she woke, touched his still strange body, and he, waking, slid his arm around her and pulled her to him. On top of him, she pressed her open mouth into his neck and rocked slowly against him, wanting to move faster but half aware all the time of the rhythmic whistling sound the nylon bag made against her skin, until finally Doug's hands, sliding down past the small of her back to hold her against him, made her forget about it. When she lifted her head and opened her eyes, she saw she had twisted her fingers into the hair just behind his ears. He was smiling at her, tears starting to fill his eyes.

"That didn't hurt a minute ago," he whispered, "but it's starting to now."

In the years since, all through grad school and these early years of their marriage, the mountains had been good to them, always reviving that first heady, infatuated desire. The problems that accumulated at lower elevations dropped away as they climbed, stayed behind with the crowds and heavy air. Above treeline, they felt they could not be touched. Like mountain goats they found their greatest protection not in the cover of woods but in the open slopes above, where, though they suffered greater exposure, they could at least see any dangers that threatened them. The analogy hadn't escaped them. "We are," they would say, smiling at each other. "We're mountain goats." They used to say it often. They said it when they went into the mountains and had fun, and they said it below too, after fights when they had made up and were laughing about things they had said. They hadn't said it much lately, though. The fights they had lately they tended not to make up.

Emily dressed and left the tent. Outside it was cold, but a brilliant morning. She dug in her pack for her down vest and put it on. She was sitting on the ground lighting the tiny campstove, her fingers cold on the metal, when Doug returned carrying his flyrod.

"Hey," he said.

He stood his pack up next to the tent and began transferring the contents of his daysack into it.

"You catch anything?" she asked. The stove was lit, and she was going through the foodbag looking for breakfast. All she could find was oatmeal.

"Nope. Some good pictures, but no fish."

"Do you ever catch any fish?" she mumbled, dropping the foodbag. Doug carried the flyrod everywhere—it had even been to Peru—but Emily had never seen him catch anything with it.

"What?" he asked.

"I said," she repeated, " 'Do you ever catch fish?' " She put a pot of water on the stove and stood up. "I'm wondering why you fish if you never catch any."

"Not often," he said. He was breaking the rod down,

47

sliding its sections into an aluminum tube. He smiled at her. "I wouldn't say never, though."

She bent down and adjusted the stove. His cheerful stubbornness irked her.

"Your problem," she said, "is you don't know when to quit."

"Hey," he replied, slipping the rod case down into his pack, "persistence pays. That's how I get to the top, you know."

They had moved to the Alps for his photography more than anything else, but it was his climbing that kept them there. The previous spring he had earned a Swiss guide's certificate. He had guided that summer and then, with some tricky winter climbs in the Alps, including an ascent of the Eigerwand and a new route of extended difficulty in the Andes, he made himself suddenly known—the other climbers all knew him, his Andean climb was written up in the journals, and now, with the climbing season starting again, clients at the guide company were starting to ask for him by name. Emily had thought it just another climb when he left for Peru, just considerably more expensive, but when he made the summit several of his friends, including the director of the climbing school he worked for, called to congratulate her, and the next day it was in the papers. It was then she realized the climbing was getting serious, that he was starting to do it for its own sake and not just to get saleable pictures. Now he had been invited on two expeditions for the fall, one in Alaska, one in the Himalayas. She had argued fiercely with him about this increased commitment to the climbing. Those sponsored trips are hard to come by, he told her, they mean a lot. So are fingers, she told him. Fingers and toes are very hard to come by. He had always climbed, but there hadn't been any talk of turning professional before they moved here. He was just trying to sell his photographs then, and climbing was a way of getting good ones. Now he was becoming known as a climber. She worried he would start to think of himself that way, and that his photography would slip away. She didn't like the idea of his going to the Himalayas. She knew the chances they took on those expeditions, setting off for summits with just a plastic bag and a few candy bars. She saw herself at home alone after work, trying not to think about it, and hearing the phone ring. They were getting into areas she didn't want to explore.

"All right," she said, checking the pot of water. "So it pays in climbing. You get to the top. But why do you keep fishing, Doug, when you never catch anything?"

He took a step back and spread his arms to the mountains about him. "It is a matter of process, my dear. It is a matter of becoming *one* with the process. One with the river, one with the rod, one with the rude, rude fish. 'Tis the journey that counts, not the journey's end."

Emily rolled her eyes. "*Don't* cite me Zen and Shakespeare," she said. "I'm a geologist. I know about process and patience. But you're not a rock, Doug. You're not even a Buddhist, for Christ's sake. People need results to look forward to. You wouldn't climb if there weren't summits. You wouldn't fish if there weren't fish. Now would you?"

Doug, who had been bouncing about on his toes and gesticulating since they started talking, stood still now, a flybox in his right hand, and stared at Emily. Emily bent down to check the water, which she found boiling. She took the pot off the campstove and dropped a teabag into it. A cinnamon stain spread through the water.

"I suppose not," Doug said. He tossed the flybox into his pack and looked at her. "But I'm not quite sure what we're arguing about."

"I don't know, either," she said, standing up again, driving her fists into the pockets of her vest. "But sometimes results are nice."

"Results?"

"Yeah. Results. I think I'd like more results out of this relationship."

"Oh Jesus," he said, looking away.

He slid his hands into his back pockets and cleared his throat.

"I'll have to ask you to define that a bit more tightly, Emily."

She looked at him, wary. He was starting to smile—a bad sign.

"You want specifics," she said.

"Yeah. Specifics."

She thought for a moment, but nothing came to mind. Doug started to move toward his pack again.

"Okay," she said, sensing she was losing him. She held up a finger. "Here's a specific. Something good to eat right now, like a trout, would be pretty nice. I think if you're going to get up early and leave me to wake up by myself when it's freezing you ought to have something to show for it."

"What about the pictures I took?"

"Those aren't for me. They don't count."

He shifted his stance a little, looked toward the river. When he looked back at her he was smiling. "Now, let me get this straight," he said. She began to smile too, despite herself. "Let me make sure I understand you correctly. You're telling me you're tired of oatmeal."

"Yeah," she nodded, laughing. "That's right. I'm getting REALLY tired of oatmeal."

"All right then," he said cheerfully, pulling his hands out of his pockets. "Good. Okay." He flipped the top of his pack shut, shoved it down to the ground with his foot and started walking toward her, an expectant grin on his face. Emily stood laughing, shaking her head.

"Oh no," she said.

"As long as we know what the issues are," he said. He opened his arms for a hug. But when he closed his arms, all he clutched to his chest was the food bag with the oatmeal in it.

After breakfast they packed up and walked east, following the streambank toward a low pass. Soon they had rounded the mountain that was on their right the day before, and were walking below its north shoulder. The trail left the streambank to wind through a stand of Norway spruce.

Amongst the trunks lay patches of snow. The fallen needles of the spruce had leaked rust-colored stains into the heavy granules, which crunched under their boots.

The trees blocked their view of the mountain. Doug could feel it before them, though, cutting off the sun, dark and massive. It seemed to him the trail should be bearing left. He pulled his compass from inside his shirt and checked it. They were walking due south, which made him think this was an approach trail to the north face. Then the trees ended and they were looking over the talus field below the face. Beyond the boulders and scree the dark granite rose craggy and rotten, smeared with patches of dark water ice, for almost two thousand feet.

"I hope the east face is better," said Emily.

"Me too."

They followed the trail east along the edge of the boulder field. Then they dropped steeply through more spruce toward the next valley. It was still early when they broke from the trees onto its meadows. The gentle slope before them was treeless except for a strip of birch bordering the stream that ran down the valley's center.

They pitched camp amongst the birch a mile downriver. The tent stood bright amongst the silver trunks. A few yards away the stream washed by. They sat on their packs sharing an orange and looked at the mountain. Doug took binoculars from his pack and scanned the face for routes. He spotted dozens.

But Emily found herself growing nervous. It had been almost nine months since she had climbed, and though she had climbed things this hard before, she felt unprepared.

"Let me see," she said. Doug passed her the glasses.

Seen through the glasses, the face didn't look so bad. The taupe-colored rock looked rough, but solid and clean, and she could see cracks and ledges and dihedrals that might let her move up the face. But when she put the glasses down and looked at it again, it looked unmanageably high and steep. She found she wasn't terribly anxious to do it.

They set out at eleven with the climbing equipment and some lunch in their daypacks. They had decided on a route slightly back up the valley from their camp. It was steep, but looked to have plenty of holds. Halfway up was an overhang split by a thin vertical crack. Beneath the overhang was a ledge. If it went well, they figured, they could be over the overhang in two or three hours, and eat a late lunch on top.

They roped up at the base of the cliff. Doug double-checked their knots and gear and set off on the first pitch. He ran out the fifty meters of rope quickly, placed some protection in a crack, and called for Emily to follow. But Emily found the route difficult. The rock was steeper and smoother, the holds more widely spaced than they had looked from the valley. Holds that looked generous from below seemed tenuous to her now. She made every move with the anticipation of falling. Between moves she stopped, frozen with indecision. As she lingered, the next move would come to seem impossible. Her legs shook from anxiety and exertion. Though she knew it was the wrong thing to do, she found herself giving in to the urge to lean forward and reduce her exposure, to feel the rock against her.

When she reached Doug at the first belay she remained silent, avoiding his eyes. She fumbled clumsily with the rope as she clipped into the belay anchors and then changed the rope over, clipping it into her belay ring. When she had doublechecked her anchor she looked briefly at him and nodded.

"On belay," she said.

Doug patted her on the shoulder. "You're not climbing all that bad, Em," he said. "You just haven't done it for a while. Relax."

She took a deep breath. "Doug," she said. "Just climb, please."

"Okay," he said, holding up his hands. "I'm going."

She paid out rope as he moved up the next pitch. The rope hummed through her belay ring. She zipped her hands back and forth in a quick rhythm, feeding it through. Twice he got ahead of her and had to ask for rope.

"I am!" she snapped the second time. "I'm feeding as fast as I can."

He slowed then, but still climbed steadily, stopping only when he reached the next belay point a fifty meters above. When he finished, Emily was breathing hard, and her hands and shoulders ached.

Back on the rock, fingers and toes. Still climbing badly, she was painfully aware of how slow she must seem after his smooth, connected moves. She made her moves tentatively, one at a time. After each move the rope rose and straightened before her, then tapped against the granite with a soft knock as Doug took up slack from above. She looked up, and he quickly looked away over the valley.

She looked down at what she was standing on, tiny flakes on the rock, and couldn't believe her feet were staying there.

All goes well if you trust your feet, Doug liked to say. He said that to his clients. It was one of his favorite climbing maxims. His favorite on the way down was more cautionary: *All the best climbers die rappelling,* he said then. She wondered if that made them angry, Doug getting them up there, setting up a rappel and then telling them that. Anyway, rappelling would come later. Right now she needed to trust her feet, and she couldn't.

Doug reached the ledge under the overhang at a little past two. It was nearly a yard wide, but he fixed some protection into the crack anyway, anchored himself, and belayed Emily as she climbed up. When she was clipped in to the anchor they took off their packs, pulled out lunch and sat back against the mountain.

"God," she said. "I'm climbing like shit."

Doug looked over the valley and tried to think of a safe response. He had become absorbed in his own climbing and in thoughts about the overhang now directly above him, and it took effort to return to a place of conversation and instruction, or even to know if that's what Emily wanted. It made him weary to think how much guessing he had to do about what she wanted lately, how much effort went into their talk. One thing he knew for sure: he wanted to finish this climb, and the way Emily was going he didn't know if she could make it. The overhang was going to be trouble.

"What's the problem?" he said. "You just weak?"

"I'm weak, I'm nervous, I'm tentative. I'm everything that makes you climb like shit."

"You need to fall."

He picked up the water bottle.

Emily knew what he meant: if she fell and he caught her, she'd realize she was safe, there was nothing to worry about. More client advice.

"That's not it," she said. "I just can't get into it. I can't loosen up."

"Maybe some wine would help. I've got some here in my sack."

He pulled out a wine bag and handed it to her.

She thought about it a minute, then squeezed a stream of wine into her mouth. The last of it hit her chin. She wiped it off with her sleeve and did it again.

"That's good," she said.

For an hour they sat on the ledge and drank wine and ate cheese and sausage and bread, saying little. At three, Doug figured they had a bit over two hours of good light left. He decided to retreat if they had much trouble with the overhang.

Emily had drunk just enough wine to remember being on a ledge like this with her brother once, looking over a valley like this one. Or maybe it was Doug, she thought; she had never climbed with her brother. She couldn't remember, wasn't even sure it happened. But this was so much like Yosemite—the clean walls, bright meadows below. She didn't see why you had to come to Europe to have this. She couldn't see, really, why they had to come here at all. People climbed in the States. It didn't make any sense.

Doug had started to put things away when she spoke. "Let's move back to Boulder," she said.

54

Doug looked down, nine hundred feet, and felt himself leaning forward. He moved back against the wall.

"What?" he said, staring at her.

"Think we could go back for the summer? I just realized I'm not real happy here. I miss it."

He stuffed the cheese into the pack.

"Em," he said. "You know I can't leave. Summer's our busiest season. I waited a long time for this job."

"Couldn't you get one there?"

"It's almost May, they'll all be gone. Besides, they're not as good there anyway. And we have a lease. We have the Alps. I thought you liked it here."

"Well, maybe just I could go," she mumbled. She picked at a loose thread on her sleeve.

Doug felt a rising panic. A tension in his stomach made it difficult to remain sitting. He sat up straighter against the rock. "What do you mean by that?" he said.

Emily shrugged. "You could see how your job goes. I could see how much I like it back home. I remember it as real great, but maybe I'm just fooling myself." She looked at him. "We have to think about going back sometime."

"Do we?"

She ignored this.

He tried a different tack. "So what if we both like it where we are?" he asked.

Emily was playing with her sleeve again, rolling the thread into little balls.

"I don't know. We could try it for a while, see how it goes. Just for the summer, probably."

From the corner of her eye she could see him shaking his head.

"Emily?"

"What?"

"When did you think this up?"

"Just now."

"Jesus!"

She looked at him. He shook his head and looked out over the valley.

"I don't understand you, Emily. I don't understand where this comes from." His lifted his hands, let them fall to his thighs. He grew more agitated as he talked. "It's crazy. You're nuts today, you know that? You won't talk to me, you're all pissed off because you can't climb, or because you *think* you can't climb, and then you spring this on me. What's the fucking deal? Where's all this come from, anyway? It is the wine, or what?"

Looking at him she wasn't sure herself. She just knew that she hated him at that moment.

"Where does this come from? I'll tell you where this comes from, Doug. From out of my brain, that's where. From out of my brain, and from getting talked to like that. It's disgusting."

"Like what?"

"Like I'm a child."

He looked back to the valley, took a deep breath and tried to calm down. He spoke as gently and thoughtfully as he could. One step at a time, like crossing a snowbridge of a crevasse.

"Look," he said. "I know we've been under a lot of strain while I'm getting started. I know you miss the States. But you've got to expect things like that. You've got to expect hard times at first. You know, richer or poorer, better or worse? I felt like things were improving lately. Don't you?"

"No."

A long silence passed.

"Then how do you see it?"

"I don't know how I see it, Doug. I'm not sure there's anything to see anymore. I feel like I know less about us all the time."

"How do you mean?"

"I don't know anything about us right now. I feel like we're just going on momentum. Like we're together just out of habit. In the habit of kissing each other, of making dinner, of making love. That's about all I know. And that when I woke up this morning I was alone. I wake up alone quite often lately. Even when you're *there* I wake up alone. I look at you and I don't know who you are anymore, who you become when you go to these ridiculous places, or why you do it, what that person has to do with me, with us. It's like you've become disconnected. Like you're adrift and floating around some *lake* or something, and I'm running back and forth on shore trying to guess where you'll land."

"You really see it that way?"

"Yes," she said.

"Well I don't feel adrift," he said. "I've never felt less so."

"You don't feel like you're adrift from me, disconnected from me?"

"Give me a break, Em," he said. "What are you—the lighthouse or something?"

"God damn it, Doug, you know what I'm talking about. I'm saying your life doesn't take me into account."

"I don't think that's true," he said, sitting back and looking away. He couldn't tell if he was lying. Maybe it just felt like he was.

"Well, I do. And I think the fact we don't see it the same way says something very disturbing. It says we're badly out of synch. Maybe if we were apart for a while we could see things better."

This made sense to him, but he didn't like it. It was happening too quickly. He lay his head back against the rock. The overhang loomed above him.

"I don't want you to leave me, Emily."

She sat up abruptly and stabbed a finger at him. "That's *just* the kind of thing I'm talking about, Doug. You haven't heard me. I didn't say anything about leaving you."

He snapped his head around and glared at her. She was surprised to see tears in his eyes. "Then what do you call it?" he said. He was almost shouting. "What do you call it when you go to a whole 'nother God-damned country?"

"I don't know," she shouted back, "I told you, I'm just thinking this out. I'm talking about an experiment, for God's sake."

"Fuck that, Emily!" He slammed his hand down onto the

pack and leaned toward her. "I don't *want* to be a fucking experiment. I want to be married, God damn it. Isn't that what we did, get married?"

He looked at her, waiting for an answer, until she turned and looked over the valley again.

Doug leaned back against the rock. What a bitch, he thought. What a bitch life is. You get married, all those promises, then some crap like where you live becomes an excuse for breaking up. Till geography do us part. For a moment he thought he couldn't stand it. He saw himself push her off the ledge. Her hair flipping upward as she vanished.

The crack was too wide for a hand jam, too narrow for anything else. Doug settled on a layback, setting his side to the mountain. He pushed on the far edge of the crack with his feet, pulled on the near edge with his hands. In this way he crept upward—a hand, a foot, the other hand, the other foot—six or eight inches at a time, his side bumping along the wall. Soon the overhang's crest pressed against his right shoulder. If he went higher, the overhang would push his shoulders out of line. He would be unable to pull against the crack, the counterforce that held him to the rock will be lost, and he would fall. How did he miss this when he was below?

He decided to take a chance. He would quit two holds at once. He would swing his outside leg, the left, up over the overhang while reaching up also with his left hand. This would put his front against the rock, his whole body sideways, spiderlike. With luck he would find something to grab.

"Be ready," he called to Emily.

He pulled hard and swung his arm and leg up over the bulge. His toes found the crack, but his hand found only smooth granite. He dug his foot in and slid his hand around looking for a hold. As he flailed around, his right leg, the one below him, began to shake under the strain. Emily, belaying him from the ledge, braced for the fall.

His right shoulder and his chin pressed painfully into the rock but he pressed them even harder, looking for extra friction. His feet, twisted into the crack, began to cramp. He clung to the rock and looked down. He was slipping, and knew he was slipping mentally as well as he began to think more of what lay below him than above. He had placed no protection yet. If he fell, he would hit that ledge or even go past it.

But fall he would, he realized. There was simply nothing here to grab.

He decided to pull his top leg down first so the overhang wouldn't kick him away from the rock and spin him out past the ledge. Then again, maybe he should miss the ledge, let the rope stop him instead of the rock. But either way, he realized, he needed to get that top foot out.

As he shifted position to do this he found, at the very edge of the overhang, lower than he had yet looked, an indentation for his left hand. A small, shallow dish, just big enough for two fingertips.

He grabbed it, pulled himself tighter to the rock. He wedged his left foot deeper into the crack above him. Then he brought his right hand up and, one finger at a time, substituted it for his left in the pocket. He could see past the overhang now, see another dish an arm's length above, a good one. He grabbed it and pulled himself up over the bulge to the safer slope above.

Stable again, resting in a crouch, Doug found he was whimpering at each exhalation. His forearms began to ache. They were just bad at first, and then they were horrible. He let himself weep. The pain seemed to flow right out through his fingertips.

Then he heard something. Emily was calling from below.

He shouted out toward the valley. He heard his voice break. It seemed tiny as it sailed out past the overhang.

"Good move," she called. "You okay?"

"Thanks," he said, and he had to laugh. What a partner, he

thought. Says she's going to leave me, then asks if I'm okay. "I'm fine."

He stood up. His breathing was close to normal again. He saw blood on his forearm and found the source on his chin, a scrape where he had dug it into the rock. But the pain in his arms was fading. He shook his hands and squeezed them into fists, shook them again. The wall above him looked easy. He was over the crux.

He turned to yell into the valley. "There's a nice little platform if you can get up here. Think you can?"

"I guess. I may need a little tension."

"All right."

He wedged a few chocks into the crack, pulled them snug, and clipped the back of his harness into their slings. Then he dropped a length of webbing to Emily and pulled up the packs.

"I'll just belay you from here, okay? That way I can pull you over if you need it."

"Okay."

"All right. You're on belay."

He stood to take the slack out of the slings holding him to the mountain. He looked over the valley. The mountain's shadow reached well past the river now, covering their camp. They would have to hurry if they wanted to make the top. He'd have to really rip the next few pitches, place minimal protection. But that was okay. The rest looked easy. It was this thing that was going to be a bitch.

"Climbing," he heard from below.

Doug checked his belay anchor once more, got a good grip on the rope.

"Climb," he said.

TINA   MARIE   CONWAY

World War II Picture

SHE HOLDS THE towel in front of her naked body, her fingers pinching tight a knot of fabric over her shoulder. In black and white, she stands smiling, her lips apart, tongue showing slightly through her straight ivory teeth—teasing, joking, drawing my eyes to the slim legs peeking out beneath the terrycloth. One knee is bent the way a majorette might pose with a baton and I can't help but run a finger over her plush thigh, down her knee, her calf to the tip of her pointed toe. She just stepped from the shower and the mirror behind her is steamy, opaque. In the rim of the mirror is a picture of Michael in uniform, the edges curled from too many, too hot showers. Her auburn hair curls around her face and falls in waves down her back

She is my mother, only nineteen, beautiful, vibrant, living in a dorm at Wayne University, dating a Warrant Officer sent overseas eight months ago. If I look at the picture hard enough I can see the tiny mole on her right temple and a faint hint of the light green eyes we share. Our noses are the same, I notice: thin; pointed; curved nostrils; and a rash of freckles over the bridge. It's her hair I wish I had. Instead, I fight with the frizzy, dark hair I inherited from my father, Michael.

She is my mother. Unaware, as she hides behind the towel, smiles for the camera, she will live to be only fifty-seven and for two of those years, the last two, she will lie in the same bed she shared for thirty-six years with my World War II hero father, the curtains drawn, a ball of cancer growing at the base of her neck. I imagined it spreading like ink dropped in water—a black cloud erupting, a muddy stain absorbing into her blood. Her face was pale and hollow. Her bones pressed to the skin and you knew each one was so fragile that with a kiss or a brush of your fingertips they might shatter, splinter to fine dust.

Each morning I watched her stand on thin, shaky legs, shuffle to the curtains, wrap her bony fingers around the cord and pull. I knew the sunlight hurt her eyes, but she stood by the window, said, "Look, there's a blue jay," or pointed to the large gardenia tree; she didn't have to say a word, we both remembered my father planting the blooming bush the day she came home from the hospital. "The weights, Amanda," she said, moving away from the window, and I'd pass her a set of hand-weights. Twenty times with each arm. She'd done this for fifteen years—along with a weekly two-mile jog, which she had long since given up— and, "you don't think I'm going to stop now, do you?" By noon, she couldn't make it to the bathroom. My father carried a shallow pie pan in from the kitchen and closed the door behind him. Before she fell asleep each night, I read a few paragraphs from *Robinson Crusoe*. She'd say, "Damnit, if I could only see the enemy, I could fight back," or she'd show me a bruise on her shin: "Battle scar. This time the culprit was none other than an open dresser drawer."

For those two years I worked the graveyard shift at the VA hospital, filing, typing, collecting and passing out magazines to the bedridden patients. My father found me the job. He went twice a month to visit the vets, gave counseling and companionship. At the time, I had just left grad school—a thirty-two-year-old divorcee who could think of nothing better to do than take classes in Ancient History—and moved home to help take care of my mother. She resented it. "Get out of the house," she said. "I know you're bored and a quick game of gin with your father isn't going to help."

I walked the halls from two to four, a stack of *Field and Stream, The Outdoorsman, Newsweek* in my arms. I knew Mr. Green liked hunting and Saul Peters would rather read *Time.* So many of the men were wide awake at four in the morning, sitting up in bed, playing solitaire, fuzzy television sets turned low. Mr. Jensen woke up when I brought his *Reader's Digest.* He confused me with his deceased wife. For thirty-nine years, every day, she brought him the magazine, read aloud "Laughter is the Best Medicine," quizzed him in "Word Power." My second day on the job I heard she had passed away in her sleep. That night when I walked into his room, he tucked the sheet around his waist and held out his hands.

"Maggie, I've missed you so much. Come, come," he said.

"Mr. Jensen, I brought your *Reader's Digest.*"

As I walked closer he reached for my hand and held it in his spindly fingers. He looked closely at the freckles on my knuckles, arms, at my pale skin, green eyes and dark hair. He knew, I think he knew, I was not Maggie, still he clutched my hand, whispered, "I dreamed about you last night. We were together in a huge green field, a pasture of flowers, and I could walk. I could curl my toes." I looked down at his feet sticking out from the sheet; white, wrinkled, the toenails long, dirty and cracked.

My mother signs the back of the picture. "Dearest Michael," she writes, her *t* crossed with an arrow, the *i* dotted with a tiny heart. "I will always be here for you. Love, Courtney." Under her name she signs the date, March 19, 1943.

Courtney takes a last look at herself, remembers her room-mate holding her new camera, yelling, "Show us some leg. Take it all off," as she stepped from the shower, and wonders if she will ever hold the picture again. She folds a piece of writing paper sprinkled with toilette water around the picture and slides it into an envelope. Playfully, she kisses the seal, leaving a wet imprint. At the post office, pushing the envelope through the mail slot, she imagines Michael's hands unfolding the paper, his thumb fingering the edge of the picture, maybe he'll bring it to his lips and on an early April morning she will awaken, from a dream of her and Michael lying on the white shores of a Pacific island, her body flushed, wrapped in a sheet and a thick wool blanket, the moist softness of a long-distance kiss lingering on her cheek.

The first time I saw the picture in my father's wallet, I was ten years old and sitting on his lap in the front porch rocker. He pulled out his credit cards one by one and each time I ran my fingers over the embossed lettering. He showed me pictures of distant aunts, uncles, and cousins I'd never met. I laughed at his driver's license picture because he looked mad and mean, and I knew that man wasn't really my father. It was an accident, I think, my father pulling out a Shell credit card and revealing my mother draped only in a towel. His face reddened. The plastic holding the picture had yellowed. I touched her hair, which I knew was long, but had never been down because each morning she stood in front of the bureau mirror and wound the greying stands into a tight bun on the top of her head.

Late one night, as I walked into his room, Mr. Jensen said, "Ask me the words, Maggie. I feel smart today."

I turned to page ninety-eight and began reading. "Eliminate. A. to develop; B. take away; C. lost; or D. to put pressure on."

"Easy one. B. to take away."

"I hear you're going into surgery soon, Mr. Jensen," I said, putting the book down. "They hope to remove some more shrapnel."

"Now, dear, there's nothing to be afraid of. We've gone through this many times." He picked up the magazine, flipped through the pages. I noticed the aqua blue of his eyes, his wavy grey hair, and, despite the deep lines on his forehead and his pale skin, saw he was a handsome man.

"Tomorrow I'll come early and we'll wheel you to the sun deck," I said, standing up. He looked up and laughed. I didn't know if he was laughing at me or a joke he had just read.

The picture travels from the mailbox in front of the Main Street, Battlecreek, post office, passes through the hands of twelve postal workers, is bundled in a canvas sack, nestling among other letters to faraway loved ones, thrown into the mail compartment of a C46 Transport that flies over the Pacific, over Oahu, the Bonin Islands, Formosa, Canton, to the 17th Group of the 447th Squadron stationed in Kunming. Twice it drops to the floor of the officer's quarters where the boot of Corporal T. R. Laken leaves a smudge of dirt just below the return address. When it reaches the hand of Michael Q. Cameron, he holds it to his face, smells the faint fragrance of gardenia, so close, so real it could be the neck, the earlobe of Miss Courtney Simmons. Unfortunately, he had cut himself shaving that morning and as he stands smiling, inhaling, a spot of blood surfaces from the wound and stains the envelope.

The second time I saw the picture I was fifteen, alone, standing in front of the wide bathroom mirror, my breasts just forming, curly dark hair growing between my legs. I was becoming like my mother. I had pulled the picture from the yellowed plastic of my father's wallet and carried it with me into the bath, holding the edge in the fingers of one hand, washing, slowly, carefully with the other, then laid it on the counter as I dried, peered into the mirror. My nipples were tender, wrinkled from the chilly air. I wrapped a towel around me like my mother in the picture, tying a knot over my shoulder, cocking my leg, pulling the corners of my mouth so high my cheeks hurt. For a moment, in the steamy mirror, my hair framing my face, my body hidden behind a thin towel, I was in love with a man at war, going to nursing school, living in an off-campus dorm, just stepping from the shower, laughing, joking, my roommate aiming the camera. For a moment, I was my mother.

Two days before she died, my mother called me to her room, patted the spread. She sat up, the pillows heaped behind her, and I saw a scarlet glow in her cheeks.

"Would you like me to read to you?" I asked.

"Tonight I will tell you a story," she said. I slid next to her and she folded her arm around my shoulder, pulling me to her. With her thin fingers she pushed my bangs across my forehead and gently urged my head to her chest.

"When your father was in Dayton, just before he left for China, I got a notice from the post office that there was a box of flowers waiting for me. I imagined a bouquet of carnations or possibly roses." Her skin was hot and I saw her hands quiver as she moved them rhythmically with the swing of her voice. "But when I got there, I couldn't even carry the box. It was full of daisies, jonquil, tulips, alstroemeria, lilies. Every flower imaginable. The post office smelled so sweet all the workers complained. 'Get those out of here, lady.' But when I held a bunch to my face all I could smell was the musty scent of your father's skin." She paused, laughed softly. "I had to go next door to the funeral home and borrow a dozen vases."

"Tell me another one," I said in a tiny voice. I am eight years old again, afraid of the dark, and my mother has lifted me from my bed, carried me to her room. I snuggled next to her while she whispers the tale of Peter Rabbit or Alice in Wonderland, my father snoring lightly beside us. This is how it should be, I thought. For too long our roles had been reversed. I was the mother unafraid of the dark, unafraid of death. My body went limp. Once again, for a long moment, I could sink into the strong warm arms of my mother.

He carries the picture in his wallet as he leaps from the transport, pulls a bloody body from the Shanghai River, slings it over his shoulder, turns and runs back. He gives the thumbs-up sign to the pilot as he scrambles through the door of the plane. Inside, he recognizes the wounded man as 1st Lieutenant Pat Walker and notices he's missing three fingers on his right hand. Michael rips open Walker's shirt, puts his ear to the man's chest. Still breathing, he thinks, then motions for the paramedic.

I didn't cry when my mother died. Instead, I pulled all the clothes from my drawers and closet and, very slowly, began replacing them, organizing each blouse, each sweater, each pair of underwear by color, season of wear, and style—peasant, yuppie, western. When that was finished, and I remember being in my room surrounded by mounds of clothing for two afternoons and part of the following evening, I went to the kitchen and started on the pots and pans. My father sat quietly, almost too still, in the rocker by the window, then, he'd stand, walk through the door and sit under the gardenia. In between papering the cabinets and reshelving the bookcase, I called Mrs. Ferguson, my mother's long-time friend, and asked her to make the necessary arrangements. By the funeral, all the rooms in the house were clean, orderly, except hers. It would be a long time before I wiped the settled dust from the surfaces of that room.

When I wheeled Mr. Jensen onto the sun deck, he squinted, threw a hand over his eyes.

"I think we'd better go in, dear. It's so bright," he said.

"Let's just sit over here in the shade." I set his brakes and pulled over a wooden bench.

"Yes, well, the sun does feel good," he said, after a few minutes. "I'm glad you came early, Maggie. I worry about you driving in the dark."

"I have something for you," I said, handing him a bag.

"The *Reader's Digest?*"

"No. Something different."

"Ah, *National Geographic.* That's wonderful. Those girls with the book carts never have any issues."

"Yes, I know," I said, noticing he was smiling, and above his upper lip was a line of moisture. "It's getting warm. Let me take that blanket off you." His legs were thin and very white, blue veins bulged through his skin.

"Hard to believe," he said, looking down at his legs. "I could walk on these two sticks at one time."

"How did it happen, Mr. Jensen?"

He leaned forward, whispered, "I'd never tell anyone but you this, Maggie. It's too shameful. The boys thought I stepped on that mine, gave me a Purple Heart, an Honorable Discharge." He stopped, looked at the wrinkled hands resting in his lap, the rigid legs, the toes he couldn't touch. "The truth is, I lost my balance on that ridge, fell head first. It was hours, I laid there hours—I couldn't move, damnit—then I heard the fighting start. Next thing I know I'm in a hospital bed."

"It's getting late," I said. "We'd better get inside."

I wheeled Mr. Jensen back to his room. In the corridors, the echo of squeaky shoes, high heels, leather soles sounded like an out-of-control machine gun, the whoosh of a flying hand grenade, shots from an M1, and I knew he heard it too.

In the barracks, lying on the top bunk, he tapes the picture on the ceiling, props his hands behind his head and remembers the last time he saw her. She stood on the crowded platform at the train station, a single daisy pulled from a handful he had given her that morning pinned behind her ear. She had wanted to tie her hair up. "Don't," he said, gathering it in his hands, running the thick mane across his cheek. "Please, don't." As the train pulled away, he watched her curls bob in the wind, fly across her forehead, her hand reaching up to brush away a loose strand, her figure becoming smaller, fainter until all he could see was her hair—a tiny red dot glowing far in the distance.

"That her?" Logan Peak asks, leaning an elbow on Michael's bunk, cocking his head toward the ceiling.
"Sure is," Michael says.

I saw the picture again and for the last time the day my mother died. We sat, my father and I, in her room, watching her breathing change from a heavy wheeze, her chest heaving, nostrils flaring, to a faint soft snoring, then, with a final pull of air into her open mouth, which she seemed to capture, hold in her lungs to possibly use later, nothing. She never opened her eyes that day, but several times her fingers twitched and she opened her palms. My father rushed to her side, drawing her hand to his cheek, whispering, "I'm here." He looked at me, added, "We're both here." After the sound of her light breathing stopped, though we knew, understood what had happened, we still sat by her bed, watching the curtains darken with dusk, twisting our hands, holding hands. My father slid the picture from his wallet, held it to the dull light from the window. He said, "I've seen dead, half-dead, men that should have been dead, their faces shot away, a leg blown off, but this, this . . ." He put his hands over his face and his shoulders trembled. I left the room.

Late at night, in the round light from the single lamp in Mr. Jensen's room, I whispered secrets, memories, crises from the past. "When I turned seventeen, I begged my mother for a car. When she wouldn't loan me the money, I sulked around the house, not speaking to her. One day I told her if she didn't buy me a Camaro, I'd move out. She just shook her head. 'I hate you. I hate you,' I yelled. She walked over to me and slapped my face." Most nights Mr. Jensen slept, his mouth drooping, his hands folded over his chest, but sometimes he'd open his eyes, search my face, then take my hand and say, "Those were hard years, dear."

She receives a telegram dated October 8, 1945. "Will arrive 3:15 train Stop October 11 Stop Battlecreek Stop Love Michael Stop." Holding the paper to her chest, she screams and falls onto the bed. "He's coming home," she cries. "He's coming home."

Mr. Jensen's room was dark and he was asleep the night I returned to work, three weeks after the funeral, and only to clean out my desk. I placed the latest copy of *Reader's Digest* on the table, sat down and put my forehead on the edge of his bed.

"My mother died, Mr. Jensen, and I'm not your wife. She's . . ." I stopped, feeling a hand on the back of my head. Without looking up. I grasped the hand and held it tight.

"I know," Mr. Jensen said.

I could feel the dampness well in my eyes, and before I knew it I was pounding my fist into the mattress, my chest heaving, my wet face buried in the sheet. Mr. Jensen pulled my face up, reached out to catch a tear hanging on my chin.

"I know, I know," he said again.

I took his hand to my lips, kissed those fingers that felt so much like the thin bones of my mother's hands

She pulls the picture from the front pocket of his uniform, holds it to the light. Yes, that's her, but now her hair is so long she can sit on the ends, her freckles have faded slightly, and she feels different, not like the young college woman who laughed and joked while her roommate snapped a picture of her semi-nude body, more like a bruised warrior, a survivor. She looks at Michael. "I didn't think I'd ever find you again," she says. That afternoon the train station had been crowded and Courtney couldn't see past the mass of bobbing heads. As the train pulled in, the crowd lunged forward, shoving, elbowing, and she was knocked into a bench, pushed off the platform. For two hours she stood by the ticket counter, waiting, watching couples embrace, families reunite, then walked slowly back home. He didn't make it, she thought. Something went wrong. As she rounded the corner, Courtney caught sight of a tall, dark man in uniform pacing the length of her front porch, a duffel bag over his shoulder.

Michael takes her hand, eases the picture from her fingers. He pulls out his wallet, says, "This kept me alive, unharmed," and slips the picture into the fresh clear plastic, where it will remain for the next thirty-six years. Possibly, from time to time, he will change wallets, pull the picture out to admire, show his daughter, hold in his palm. She stands ready, this image of my mother, frozen, preserved in youth, the soft green eyes, long hair, gentle smile—ready to fight, to wait, to always be here.

Midway

MY FATHER TOLD me not to answer the door. He said it was the deputies knocking again, trying to serve a paper from my mother for "non-support." And while the fist rattled the painted glass in the top of the living room door, he sat quietly across from me at the other end of the warped plyboard table in our kitchen, smoking a cigarette and cocking a nervous ear toward the racket. When I fidgeted in my chair, he winked at me and put a hushing finger to his lips.

Three meals' worth of unwashed dishes divided the table between us. There were empty vegetable cans and potted meat cans scattered among the plates, empty cracker cellophanes and a torn bank envelope full of returned checks. Pale autumn light filtered through a pair of broken window louvers beside the table, showing the creases around my father's eyes as he stirred bourbon slowly into his coffee with a sardine key.

"Do you realize, Hank," he whispered, "what sort of man that is out there?" He pointed with his cigarette toward the living room. A broad hat threw a shadow against the door glass. Static and broken voices sputtered from a walkie-talkie on the man's hip. The sound of the knocking was loud in the living room because there was no furniture in there now. We had moved it all into the rear den a week ago when the deputies first started to visit. My father thought this might make the place look vacant. He thought it might make the deputies believe we had moved.

But the strategy hadn't worked, and for three days straight now these men had come knocking. They stayed for half an hour sometimes, kicking around in the leaves outside, then they left. It was all very predictable, but these visits frightened my father, and lately he had begun to talk of really moving, of slipping away in the night to some corner of Montgomery where they couldn't find him. But I knew this was nothing but talk. This little house on Teague Street south of the interstate belonged to my father's friend Mr. Easely. We didn't have to pay any rent on it, and that was about as much rent as we could afford. My father made a little money driving a route west of town, collecting cash insurance payments from old black women and sorghum farmers, but he spent most of this money in the bars. We were too broke to move, and I knew it. We were here for the duration, whatever that might turn out to be.

We were here because of a fight that had happened at my mother's house out in Bonnie Crest. For over a year, my father had been unemployed (after he lost his Life of Alabama agency when he couldn't meet quotas), and since that time my mother had been the only provider in our house, selling real estate. For a while she took this in stride. My grandfather had willed her the house, and she took another mortgage on it. She paid my father's bar bills at the country club and believed him when he said he was looking for work. But gradually, she grew tired. She began to complain about my father's drinking. She cut him off at the club when we were down to eating meat only once a week, and she demanded that he find a job.

Then she caught him using one of her credit cards to finance a three-day drunk with Mr. Easely and her tolerance was finished. She screamed. She accused. She broke all his liquor bottles in the bathtub and my father packed. He made me carry his golf clubs out to the car, then told me to climb inside with the bag. My mother and three sisters cried and beat on the car windows, but I went with him. I went because I had always been told that it was right for a boy to obey his father. That was six weeks ago. I hadn't seen my mother or sisters since.

"Well, I'll tell you what kind of man it is," my father whispered, pointing again at the shadow in the top of the door. "I'll tell you this." He took a drink from his coffee cup and gritted his teeth. "You don't get to be a deputy in Montgomery County," he said, "by spending all your Sundays in church." He smiled at me and squeezed his cracked bottom lip.

He had been shaving when the knocking first began, and his face was still spotted with foam now as he smoked thoughtfully, using the scrambled eggs he hadn't eaten for breakfast as his ashtray. I knew I should tell him about the foam. He would be leaving soon to start his route. But I didn't tell him. He hated being reminded of things he had forgotten, and I didn't feel much like suffering one of his bourboned stares.

"They're a slippery school of fish all right," he whispered, flavoring his coffee again with the whiskey. He smiled and tapped the sardine key against his brow. "But they're no club of geniuses either," he said. "We won't let them lock the old man up, just because your mother's gone a little jealous."

I shook my head at this. My father always liked me to agree when he talked about my mother's being jealous. She was still in love with him, he told me. Even after all she had accused him of being and not being over the years, she still kept a coal red for him in her heart. That was what made her so dangerous. She couldn't abide the idea of his running free without her. She was exchanging ropes for chains, my father said. She loved him so much that she wanted him thrown in jail.

"No sir," my father said, taking another pull at his cup.

"She can send these bastards knocking till their hands bleed. I'll never give her the satisfaction of seeing me in front of a judge."

He took a hard drag from his cigarette and blew the smoke against the wall. He thought I was offended by the habit, though I was already pilfering butts out of his ashtrays when he wasn't around. The tobacco was always harsh. It made me feel dirty and sad. But I smoked it anyway, all the way down until the filter got hot between my lips. I liked it, though it tasted bad. I liked it in the same secret way I liked the cans of Falstaff I sometimes stole from the refrigerator and drank while my father was asleep. His smoking made me want a drag myself, and I wished he would hurry up and leave.

The knocking continued out front, though the intervals were growing longer between each blow. We didn't really have anything to worry about anyway, as I understood it. The deputies couldn't serve you a summons so long as they didn't meet you face to face, and the only way they could get into the house was with a search warrant. My father had explained all these rules to me several times. He wanted to make sure I knew the score about our rights. My mother might hold the aces because he owed her money, but as long as we were careful, we still had a few trump cards up our sleeves.

"There," my father whispered when the screen door fell back against the house. The shadow of the hat was gone and leaves crunched under boots along the walk. The kitchen was quiet except for the drip of the coffee pot and the rush of the trucks along the interstate in front of the house. My father smiled at the silence. He crushed the last of his cigarette out in his eggs.

"Saddle up," he told me. "I've got a job for you this morning." I followed him down the hall, across the packing quilts he had laid over the floor to muffle our steps. When we reached my room in the back of the house, he sat down on my cot and pulled on a pair of socks. He never put his shoes on when he believed the deputies were watching until just before he crept out the back of the house after his car, which he parked in a church lot a few blocks south. He wasn't risking any foul-ups, he said. If the deputies heard so much as a heel squeak inside our place, they might stay outside watching till we starved. Like soldiers in a siege. That was the kind of men my mother had working for her, he said. Heartless bastards, these county men. He filled his pocket flask with bourbon.

"We have to work quick now," he said, "Your mother knows people. Her father had friends at the courthouse." He wrapped himself in a dark overcoat and pulled a water-stained fedora down low on his face. "It won't take her long to get those badges a warrant," he said, "if that's what she wants." He handed me a paper sack from the pocket of his overcoat and opened the back door.

"You get that to Mr. Easely before nine o'clock." he said, pointing at the sack. "It's very important." He gave me a cold handful of quarters to cover bus fare.

"Nine o'clock," he said again, crouching in the leaves that covered the back stoop. I could feel it was chilly outside. The pecan trees in the yard were stripped bare, and a cold wind stirred their branches against the roof. In my bare feet, I shivered. But even in the cold, my father had begun to sweat. Shaving cream dripped from his chin to the breast of his coat as he took a quick drink from his flask.

"Don't worry," he said, giving me a wink. "They couldn't catch me with a troop of hounds." He turned an ear to the wind, listening one last time for the law, then he was gone. Running low and fast, he disappeared behind a neighbor's drying laundry. I went to his golf bag in a closet where I kept my store of cigarette butts hidden in the ball pocket, and I had myself a smoke.

Mr. Easely was our family attorney and my father's best friend. Once he had been a business lawyer in one of the big firms down by the capital, but he had been "asked to leave" that position last spring when one of the partners (a Baptist "snake handler," to hear Mr. Easely tell it at the time) had smelled rum on his breath at a contract hearing. He had a small office on Heustess Street now, in one of the shabby neighborhoods below Mt. Meigs Road, where he probated wills and ended marriages for the working people around Capital Heights. The office was above a shop where Mr. Easely repaired and sold sewing machines whenever his practice was lagging, and as I started north under the interstate on the number eleven bus that morning, this was where I expected to find him, since his practice had been lagging now for quite some time.

Mr. Easely's wife Dinah had divorced him a few months before because he drank too much, because he had friends like my father who drank too much, and because he couldn't keep away from a certain group of women who frequented the cellar lounges down along Highland Avenue—women who also drank too much, women who (according to Dinah whenever she used to come out to Bonnie Crest to help my mother fret) had often signed Mr. Easely's credit card receipts in the past.

Since this divorce, Mr. Easely spent very little time in his law office. My father had been his only legal client in weeks, and he used the room above his shop now more as a place to sleep than as an office for giving counsel. But despite this turn in fortune, my father said that Mr. Easely was still lucky in one respect. He had no children, no legal wards, so his wife couldn't get some judge to squeeze him penniless with a bunch of lies, as my father said my mother would squeeze him if she ever got him inside the courthouse.

But Mr. Easely never looked as though he felt very lucky to me. Since he started sleeping in his office, he only looked tired. His eyes were dry and slow to move, and he had lost a lot of weight. All his suits bagged now at the shoulders and the waist, and his wedding band and his college ring slipped loose between the knuckles of his long fingers as they worked slowly around the belts and gears of his sewing machines.

And lately, his fingers had also begun to shake quite a lot. His eyelids had begun to spasm, and his skin had turned a dull ashen color. He seemed to age ten years in the space of three or four weeks—all since he had decided to quit the bottle.

He was reforming himself, trying to save his own life. That was what Mr. Easely said with a tired smile each time my father asked him out for a drink at the Banjo Cabin or the Tin Pail. For more than an hour sometimes, I would stand around the shop, watching the men smoke together while my father tried to convince his old friend to give up his "useless sacrifice."

"Hell, man," my father would say. "Dinah doesn't care a stump what you do anymore. Not since she got your house." Looking around at the dusty sewing machines that cluttered the display floor, he would shake his head. "Why're you wasting your time in this morgue? I've got credit with Cecil and Mr. Larry. Why don't you come downtown?"

But no matter how old the promised Scotch, no matter how inviting the descriptions of hot bar sausages and pickled eggs (which often made even my own mouth water), Mr. Easely always answered by shaking his head. He tried to pass his refusals off lightly, claiming a sour stomach or a backlog of work, but it was always clear to me that he was tempted. The thirst was always bright in his eyes. Yet every time we visited his shop now, we left it without him, and I would go alone with my father to watch him salt his beer in the dark rooms of taverns.

I thought of that look in Mr. Easely's eyes again as the doors of the number eleven bus folded shut behind me at the corner of Ann and Geneva Streets, and I touched my father's package inside my windbreaker pocket. I had an idea about what was inside this paper, and I knew Mr. Easely wouldn't like it. I tried to come up with some scheme or excuse to get out of delivering it, but then a police car stopped to idle at the intersection, and I turned quickly away toward Heustess Street.

I saw Mr. Easely through the broad glass front of his shop. He sat at his workbench in the back of the paneled show-room, playing with the belt motor out of an old Singer machine. He smiled when I tapped against the display glass.

"Hello, Hank," he said, standing as I pushed through the front door. I shook his hand and his rings were cold. His fingernails were chewed and scabbed at the quicks. "On your own this morning?" he asked, looking back through the display window. He seemed relieved when he saw my father wasn't following.

"On an errand," I said, and I quickly handed him the paper sack. It made me nervous, meeting Mr. Easely alone this way. Ever since he left the bars, he had become very serious. He stared at me all the time. He asked me about school, about grades, and he looked worried whenever he found out I was skipping classes again, like today. Before, when he was still drinking with my father, he had been quite a jolly guy. He was always quizzing me with riddles, stabbing me playfully in the ribs with the olive swords out of his martinis. But now all that was gone. His smiles were forced and he hardly ever laughed. His sober eyes made me nervous, and already I felt anxious to get away from the shop.

"You know I'm glad you stopped in, Hank," Mr. Easely said. "I've been wanting to talk to you." He fingered the edges of the paper sack carefully, and I could tell he was a little worried about opening it. His eyes were red and dull. He looked as though he hadn't rested in days. "I've been wanting to talk to you alone," he said. "About your father. About you living with your father."

"He told me you need to look at that before nine o'clock," I said, pointing at the bag. "He says it's very important." Mr. Easely stared at me for a few moments without a word. It was clear he didn't want to change the subject, but when I pointed again, he nodded slowly and tore open the stapled mouth of the sack. He shook his head when he found a letter inside, taped to a little bottle of Frontier Gin.

"Jesus," he said, putting the bottle down on his workbench. "Jesus," he said again, and we both stared at the bottle, at the grinning face of an Indian on its label. Mr. Easely stepped away from the bench and turned his stare on me.

"You knew what was in that bag all along," he said. "Didn't you, Hank?" I looked at the worn carpet at his feet. "And you brought it anyway," he said. "Jesus." He fumbled a cigarette out of his shirt pocket and nearly burned himself lighting it.

"I think the note is what's important," I said quietly. "I think it has something to do with the law." I pointed at the envelope that was taped to the side of the bottle. My father had printed the word "URGENT" across the seal.

Mr. Easely sighed. He took several quick pulls from his cigarette, eyeing the bottle, then stepped forward and ripped the note away. He stepped back just as quickly, letting an ash fall from the cigarette on his chest. His hands shook as he cut the seal with a pocketknife.

"We aren't finished talking yet, Hank," he said. Even his forced smiles were gone now. He took the letter to the front of the shop, as far away from the bottle as he could get. To keep from meeting his eyes, I looked around the showroom.

There were two stuffed rainbow trout on the wall nearest the workbench, and between the fish there was a photograph of Mr. Easely and my father. In the black and white picture, the men were young and they both wore rubber chest waders and crewcuts. They stood with flyrods in the shallows of a river pool, smiling back at the camera with cigars between their teeth. The photograph was very old, taken before either of the men was married. Neither Mr. Easely nor my father went fishing anymore. I had never been fishing myself.

Mr. Easely coughed on his cigarette smoke, standing among the rebuilt machines he was trying to sell in the window. And as he shook his head above my father's note, I saw the pink of his scalp where his hair was thinning in back. His shoulders were stooped and he had to hold the paper close to his face to read. Watching him there in the dusty light, it was hard to believe he had ever stood in a river. He shook his head again and I looked at the gin bottle, wishing I had dropped the damned thing in his mailbox and run away. I tried not to look at the face of the Indian again.

Stapled against the paneling on the other side of the room was a bright red and blue poster advertising the county fair which had its run that week. On the poster, a little boy and girl ate cotton candy and held balloons. A young man in a letter jacket cradled his girlfriend's shoulders in his arm, leading her toward the lighted spokes of the ferris wheel. And in the blue ink at the bottom of the page, a man in a wide-crowned hat threw baseballs at the wooden faces of clowns.

The poster reminded me of Bonnie Crest, of my mother's house out near the fairgrounds and the many autumn nights in the past when I had walked in the sawdust of that midway. My mother and sisters didn't care much for the sort of people who gathered at the fair ("trailer trash," they called them), and my father was rarely around to take me. So I would go alone to ride the Scorpion and the Bullets, to wager pennies for candy on the Gypsy Wheel, to watch the strange man who ate colored glass. Then, when my stomach was full of candied corn and my money was gone, I would walk home across the links of the country club, finding my mother cracking her knuckles on the sofa, cross and nervous because my father hadn't come home from work.

"Hank," Mr. Easely said sharply. "What are you staring at?" His voice brought me back from Bonnie Crest, and I realized my eyes were fixed on the bottle of gin. When I turned, Mr. Easely was halfway across the room, and there was a hard look in his eyes. His face was even paler than before, and he held my father's note clenched in his fist. When he reached the workbench, he rummaged through a drawer and brought out two chipped Collins glasses.

"If I have a drink of this, Hank," he said, "would you like to join me?" There was a little refrigerator underneath the workbench, and from this he brought out a tray of ice and a lemon.

"What are you talking about?" I asked. "What are you saying?" I knew it had to be some sort of trick, but my words didn't stop him.

"If I promised not to tell your father," he said, "would you like to have some of this gin?" His hands worked with practiced movements, dropping two cubes of ice into each of the Collins glasses, quartering the lemon with his pocket-knife. When everything was ready, he set the bottle down between the tumblers and looked up at me.

"Would you like that, Hank?" he asked. "If I swore no one would ever find out?"

I hesitated this time. It was a ridiculous idea, but Mr. Easely seemed completely serious, staring at me as he broke the tax seal around the bottle's cap. I started to dismiss the offer, to ask him what the hell he was trying to do. But I didn't. The tumblers looked so cool, sweating already against the bench face. The smell of the cut lemon made my mouth water. I listened to the ice pop as it melted in the glasses. I looked at Mr. Easely and didn't tell him not to pour.

He blinked at me several times. His eyes shifted back and forth, looking hard into each of my own. He rubbed his mouth on the back of his hand, then nodded.

"One thing first, though," he said quietly, after a long pause. He smoothed my father's note on the bench and held it out for me. "Read this," he said. "That's all. Do that and we'll have a drink."

I looked at the paper, but I kept my hands at my hips. I didn't want to read it. I didn't want to think about my father just now. I looked at the Indian on the gin bottle, but Mr. Easely shook the note in my face.

"Read it," he said, and I took the paper by the edges. The writing was scrawled and the ink was smeared in places by drops of sweat, but I began to make it out.

"They're out there," was all it said, over and over again, a dozen times.

"They're out there." And at the bottom of the page, my father had drawn a picture of a stick man, standing on a gallows with a rope around his neck. "She wants this to be me," he had written beneath the drawing, with an arrow pointing from the words to the man in the rope.

I dropped the paper on the floor. I pushed it away with my shoe. Mr. Easely leaned toward me.

"You know the truth, Hank, don't you?" he asked softly.
"You know you have to leave your father. He's lost, and if you
stay there with him, he'll lose you too." He touched my chin
and turned it so I had to look at him. His arm was shaking and
his eyes were squinted as they watched me. "You know,
Hank, don't you?" he whispered. "It isn't your father those
deputies want."

"I have to go," I said, pulling out of Mr. Easely's grip. He
didn't try to stop me. He didn't move. There was another fair
poster stapled to the inside of the street door, but I kept my
eyes away from it. I jerked the door open and started quickly
toward the bus stop.

I saw Mr. Easely again as I passed in front of the display
window. His hands were folded on the workbench near the
Collins tumblers, and he was staring at the little bottle of gin.

When my father burst through the back door of the
kitchen that night, he went directly to the stack of mail I had
picked up from our post office box that afternoon. I was
playing cards with myself at the other end of the table, using
only a candle for light so the rest of the house would remain
dark. My father didn't seem to notice me as he sorted
through the envelopes, dropping bills unopened on the
floor. He was looking for some word from my mother, as he
did every night—some letter pleading for him to come back
to her house. But there was nothing. My mother never wrote
him any letters. She only wrote to me, asking *me* to come
back to Bonnie Crest, and I always hid these notes before he
had a chance to see them. When his hands were empty, my
father looked up at me for the first time.

His eyes were glazed red in the shifting candlelight. He
watched my hands move the playing cards, matching clubs
on diamonds, red on black. The shaving cream was gone
from his face, but his jaw was still gray with stubble. I could
smell the bourbon on his breath from the other side of the
room. He picked the bills up off the floor, then dropped
them again. He stared at me and rubbed his chin.

"Go to bed," he told me suddenly. He blew out the candle flame and felt his way along the walls to the back of the house. I heard him dialing the telephone in the den where all the living room furniture was stacked, then his voice talking low into the mouthpiece. "Please, Hank," he called to me. "Please go to bed."

An hour later there was a knock against the door of my room. Afraid of deputies, I pushed myself deep under my pillow. A pair of fingernails scratched along the door, and the springs of my father's bed expanded in the next room.

"Open it," he called in a flat voice from behind his door. I slipped the bolt free, and a woman in a white nurse's uniform stumbled inside with the cold. She looked at me closely as her eyes adjusted to the darkness of the house. I recognized her from the Tin Pail where my father often bought her drinks. She wore heavy makeup and a thick moustache grew in each corner of her mouth. She carried a bottle of whiskey by its neck, and she laughed at me in my underwear while she worked a lipstick from her purse and colored her mouth.

"Hello, little convict," she whispered, slurring each word. "Has the warden taken all your clothes?" I shook my head, smelling her lemon perfume and the whiskey on her breath. The woman laughed at my staring eyes as she blotted her lips on a match folder. She kissed me on the nose, and I saw lipstick caked in the hairs of her moustache.

I felt an urge to touch the hairs. I was afraid of the woman, but her face was close and warm, and I felt an urge to touch it all. I leaned forward, hoping she might kiss me again, but she stood up and opened my father's door. The neck of the whiskey bottle clicked several times against the mouths of glasses in there, and in a few minutes, the nurse's low noises began.

The sounds frightened me in a way I didn't quite understand. They made frightening things move inside of me, and I felt an urgent need to get away. Dressing quickly, I went to the hall. I pulled down the ladder from the ceiling while the woman's voice grew louder behind my father's door. I climbed up into the hot darkness of the attic, then through a window that opened onto the roof.

The sounds weren't so loud here as before, but I could still hear the woman's cries and the quickening springs below me. A part of me wanted to listen closely, to hear every turn of the nurse's voice. But then I remembered that it was my father down there, and the noises made me angry and ashamed. He had never brought one of these women to the house before, and I cursed him now for making me listen to such a thing.

Closing the window behind me, I lay with my belly against the roof shingles and scanned the street and driveways for deputy cars. I decided no county men were watching tonight, and I looked north toward Bonnie Crest where the lights of the fair would be making the sky red above my mother's house at that hour. Moving beams from the headlamps of the cars along the interstate picked through the limbs of the pecan trees waving above the yard. The car tires made a ringing sound against the pavement as they moved.

And as I lay there against the roof, with the rhythm of the nurse's voice climbing beneath me, I wished I could be with the people in those cars, or at the fair, at least—lost among a crowd of strangers. I wanted to smell the sawdust in the midway, to touch the animals in the farm contests, to feel the diesel heat from the engines of the rides. I wanted to hear the high school girls laughing with their boyfriends and the barkers shouting promises about their shows. I wanted to ride the Spider and the Vertigo, to shout through the Tomb of Frights—anything to escape the way I felt just then. I wanted to sit on top of the ferris wheel with all the bright pinnacle stars and never go home anywhere ever again.

But instead I stayed there on the roof, cursing my father with my eyes closed until I heard the back door open and shut. The nurse walked a bicycle into the front yard, singing to herself. She stopped to light a cigarette in the driveway, coughing several times, and she checked her face in the mirror of a compact. Then she was gone, pedaling easy down our street, swaying through the blinking mica in the pavement.

I climbed back through the window and crawled carefully over the lumber bracing toward the ladder. I thought of calling Mr. Easely tonight. I wanted to tell him I was ready to leave, that I couldn't go on living this way anymore. But as I passed above my father's room, I heard noises still below me. I pulled away a strip of insulation and put my ear to the ceiling board.

My father was crying beneath me. I heard him pour another glass of whiskey, then he shouted and threw the glass against the floor. His weeping grew louder and he said my mother's name several times. He began to pray, to call my mother's name over and over again in a frightened voice of prayer. He asked God to help him, to save him, to deliver us all from this hell He had made of Montgomery. Then he called my sisters' names and he threw himself on his bed.

His sobs grew quieter, and gradually I heard his hoarse breathing slow into sleep. He coughed once or twice, then began to mumble with dreams. I climbed downstairs and let the ladder up quietly. I went to bed with my clothes on and pulled my blanket tight around my chest. Then I lay awake for a long time, staring at the faded spots on the wall where another tenant family had once hung its photographs.

I woke with a hand over my mouth, shaking my head back and forth until I pulled up slowly from a dream full of singing women and police sirens and guns. It was my father's hand, and it trembled as it held my lips shut. His eyes were red and wild as he jerked me from my blanket and set me on the floor. His breath was already stinking with bourbon. He pointed toward the living room through the hall.

"She got the bastards a warrant," he whispered, brushing my ear with his hot lips. "I heard them talking," he said. "God only knows how many there are out there."

He wore only his boxer shorts and a pair of unlaced boots. He held a golf club, a four wood, close to his throat, and sweat streamed down his face, clinging with flecks of cigarette ash in his eyebrows and his three-day beard.

"Come on," he whispered, and he pulled me into the kitchen. The nurse's whiskey bottle stood empty on the table beside a saucer heaped with cigarette butts, and there were sheets of paper scattered over my hand of solitaire where my father had been trying to write a letter. He squatted to keep his profile hidden beneath the windows, and I could hear his chest whistling as he held me firmly at his waist.

"What a woman your mother is," he said. He wasn't whispering any longer, and his voice grew steadily louder as he spoke. He forced me to squat beside him in the living room door, but he didn't look at me. His legs were shaking. "How could she be so damned jealous?" he asked. "How could she really want these bastards to throw me in jail?" His eyes searched around the walls of the living room, leaping from one window to the next. His fingernails made white cuts in the skin on my arm. A car door slammed shut out on the street.

"Ahhh," my father said, gritting his teeth. "Christ, she's really doing this." Feet rustled in the leaves outside. Somebody called my father's name. "Ahhh," he said, pressing the shaft of the golf club against his chest. His sweat made dark spots in the dust on the floor. "It's crazy," he said. "To think I've driven her to this."

"The back door," I whispered. "We can still get out the back door." I pulled his shoulder and pointed toward the rear of the house. "We can go to Mr. Easely's," I said. "We can hide in his office."

But my father didn't seem to have heard me. It was as though he had lost all sense that I was there with him in the room. His entire body was shaking now, but it wasn't fear that was making him tremble. His eyes were bright and full of heat. A strange smile pulled at the corners of his mouth. His throat began to move with silent laughter as a voice again called his name in the yard. He was shaking with excitement, I realized.

"Dad," I whispered. "Dad, we've got to get out of here."

But again he didn't seem to hear me. His laughter rose up in a low chuckle, and he let go of my arm.

"By God," he said, blinking as sweat ran into his eyes. His voice sounded calm and far away. "By God," he said again. "This is what she wants." I tried to grab his shoulder again, but he pulled away. He began to squat across the living room with the four wood in his lap.

"Dad," I called in a loud whisper. "What are you doing, Dad?"

But my father was alone now, it seemed. He stood up and faced the front door where a hand had begun to knock. He held the golf club firmly across his chest. "By God," he said, talking to the painted window glass. "If this is what she wants, then I'll give it to her." He took hold of the door knob and the fist let off with its knocking outside. "Then we'll see who's a coward," he said. "Then we'll see who's nothing but a drunken fool."

I ran forward and grabbed my father's elbow. "Think!" I tried to shout, but my throat wouldn't work. "Think!" It came out in a whisper. I punched at my father's knees while he opened the door. He looked down at me for a moment, but not at my eyes. He looked at my hair, at my shoulders, at my legs dragging beneath me on the floor. It was as though he were looking at me in a photograph taken long ago, as though I had already become part of all those things he would regret.

"It's what she wants, Hank," was all he said to me. "It's what she wants." He swung his arm and tossed me back into the living room, hitting me in the nose with the grip of the club. Then he was gone. The copper smell of pain filled my nose, and I covered my head with both arms, waiting for gunshots.

But there was no shooting outside. There were no shouts. The screen door clapped slowly shut, and I felt blood run from my nostrils to my lip. I waited for screams, for cursing, for the blow of clubs. But there was nothing.

I picked myself up slowly from the dust in the center of the room and looked out at the driveway that was framed in the door. The wind stirred brown and yellow leaves across the pavement. The limbs of the pecan trees scratched against the roof.

Across the street, I saw a neighbor man on his porch, shading his eyes with his palm as he stared toward our yard. Two children stood beside him, pointing until the neighbor man pushed down their arms. The man turned away and shook his head. He gathered his family back inside his house. I walked forward and put my face against the cold screen door. I looked where the neighbor children had been pointing.

My father sat in a corner of the yard with the four wood between his outstretched legs. He stared across the street at the rush of the interstate. There were no deputies, no warrants, no county men. There was only Mr. Easely sitting in the leaves beside my father. He had the little bottle of Frontier Gin, and he was pouring it out evenly into two paper cups.

"Here, boy," Mr. Easely said as I approached. He put a mound of silver coins in my hand. He pointed at my lip and I wiped the blood away with the sleeve of my shirt. My father didn't look up at me as I stood over him. He just stared at the freeway, beginning to shiver as his sweat dried in the wind. Mr. Easely took off his jacket and put it around my father's neck.

"Go home, boy," Mr. Easely said. "Go get the bus for Bonnie Crest." My father said nothing to this. He only turned the wooden head of the golf club in the leaves at his feet. Mr. Easely lit a cigarette and put it between my father's lips.

"Go home," Mr. Easely said again. He had dark spots, like bruises, under each of his eyes. He looked as though he hadn't slept in weeks. He saw me staring at the paper cup in his hand and his face went hard. He looked away and pointed north up Teague Street. He didn't look at me again.

"Go home, Henry," he said. "Go home, son. Your father won't have any more trouble with deputies."

I waited for my father to speak, to say that I couldn't go,

that I had to stay with him there in our little house forever. But he said nothing. He only stared and twisted the grip of the golf club in his lap. I watched his thin hair turn in the wind, and then I started walking.

I set my eyes on a stop sign at the end of the block and I took big strides. At every step, I listened for my father's shout. I waited for him to run and grab me by the arm, to hit me for thinking I could go. But when I turned at the corner, he was still sitting with Mr. Easely in the leaves. He still stared straight ahead at the traffic, but he was nodding now as his old friend raised his cup.

MARTY   LESLIE   LEVINE

Light in My Pocket

MY FATHER WALKS like a visitor in his own house. He stares at
the bookshelves, at the clutter from another time. He bumps
into tables, he ducks under hanging plants and lampshades,
surprised. Suddenly a tourist in his own life. Wake up,
Milton. I want him to take charge. He's got the size for it—
walking behind him normally you'd never know you could
deal with him. Not for him the old-man gait—pants baggy
like a second skin falling behind with each step; no sir.

But look at his face and you realize anything is possible.
The scrubbed pink of it and the straight, combed-back hair
reduce his size. He becomes altogether manageable; a
talker, not a doer. Ultimately soft. He is across the room, at
the window to the back yard, surveying the lawn, the land-
scaping, the neighbors as if considering the house for
purchase—this house which saw thirty-two years of his life.
Ten months ago Rayma wanted a separation—Milton didn't
protest. Marriage cancelled, like the Sunday paper and the
phone service. House paid up, child gone, dog long buried,
end of show. Welcome to the curtain call.

Such a crazy divorce is about to take place. And Rayma announced it to me at her father's funeral. Funny thing, a funeral—too formal to begin with, people deferring to each other as if they were out on prom night; soon enough, though, they break into honest chaos: the uncle before his heaping plate, the neighbor tossing in business affairs, the children retreating to laugh by themselves. The eating, after the burying, the numb shovelling of food which signals to the living that life continues, took place in this house for a week after Zeyde's funeral. The assembled, suited, worked-up mix of family sweated in the living room while I escaped down the hall. But Rayma found me that first night, and made her announcement.

After a life of doing everything expected of them my parents fell down so clumsily. "An act of bravery," Rayma called it recently, on the crackling phone line from her sister's house in West Virginia. "You shouldn't take it so hard, Willy," she said: "We set you out in the world in fine shape. You moved away years ago—you have a nice apartment. We can be your parents without living together."

Makes them damn inconvenient to visit, though. You think of such practical things amid the emotional chaos, as if the mind had a separate account for these items, mechanically totalling up interest. Life wanders, but you keep track of it all. Everything is a distraction. Shifting, steering, swerving to avoid a child on the street, you think of last week's golf game with nostalgia. During sex part of you is bagging groceries and marvelling at the bill. Practical. That's what today is all about, the practical side, splitting up the home into two households. I am to provide a Solomonic solution, to baby my parents through the process.

"Your mother and I can't decide what to do with the house things, Willy," my father said one night last month during his weekly call. "You go, see, take what you need—go look in your cupboard, there are things in there from twenty years ago you haven't cleaned out. Make it a little easier for us, Willy."

No one flies three thousand miles to clean out a cupboard. "I'll come see you, Dad," I said over the phone. "I'll rent a car at the airport, you won't have to do a thing."

"And you'll decide what you want from the rest of the house," Milton said. The big shot, trying to give away his life.

"Is this a going-out-of-business sale?"

"You got your sarcasm from your mother," Milton said.

"I don't need to get anything from the house, Dad."

I don't need anything at all but some explanations. Someone has put a curse on us. My family, all three of us, talk and talk and come to temporary understandings. Explanations stand side by side neatly like teeth, but we still remain mysteries to each other.

The doorbell sounds, and Milton looks at me. He could never answer the phone either, or walk down the hall to ask Rayma for anything. "Go get your mother," he'd say. He doesn't have to say anything this time.

I kiss Rayma awkwardly on the cheek as she struggles through the door with empty suitcases. "Is there more?" I say, but she sets the leather cases smartly on the carpet and turns to me beaming. I know she has taken over the house, and the day.

In the ninth grade I was finally tall enough to look Rayma in the eye. Since then I have gained another foot and Rayma has begun her return to the elements, her hair like straw from the chemicals she puts into it, eyes sunk in water, skin like paper, smooth but flimsy on her cheek when I kissed it. But since I've grown past her she has only gained power. Children, she feels, need protection—adults, I have found out, have to fend for themselves. A week ago I called her:

"Momma, I talked to Dad the other night." Static on the line from Snowshoe, as if my mother were buried under three feet of snow. "Did you hear me?"

"So what did he have to say, Willy?"

"Mom, he said do you want the toaster oven or the microwave, which one, because he wants at least one."

"Either, I don't care." A pause. I could picture her looking away. "Is that all?"

"He says he likes his apartment."

"Why shouldn't he like his apartment, it is very nice," she said.

"I think he misses you."

"You think?"

"He told me."

"Which does he miss more, the microwave or the toaster oven or me?"

This time I couldn't reply. I had to be cautious with Rayma. I had to say the truth but with sarcasm, always with things a little sideways to let my mother add in the harder parts.

"Okay, he misses me," Rayma said. "Well, I miss him—a bit. Sometimes."

"Should I tell him?"

"Do what you want."

"I want to tell him."

"Fine." I heard what must have been the telephone changing hands, or the seat shifting around. My mother exhaled heavily: I could almost see the lines down her cheeks relaxing. "Look, tell him he can call me once in a while, Sylvia won't hang up on him I promise. Tell him however it is too late to act like a gentleman, she knows everything there is to know about him."

If I were still a child Rayma would have sat me down long before this and explained Milton's terrible faults to me. Whatever they were, these differences that turned her husband into something less than a man after thirty years—that make her face me now with such a smile in the dusty surroundings of her abandoned life, a smile for me and not for Milton—whatever mistakes he made still hang in the air like a building stuffed with dynamite, the second after the button is pushed. Already it is fragments, plaster, dirt and noise—only our eyes hold it together in the air.

Milton steps up beside me and pokes his chin at Rayma's cases. He blinks at Rayma's tailored suit. "You look well," he says. She looks—difficult. She looks like a sudden obstacle in the road. And she looks tired, though she hides it well behind a bluster of speech.

Am I unfair? Does Rayma force me to make these judgments because she so pointedly treats me like any other adult? Do I become one of her swim-club mates, those made-up old ladies in bathing suits at the card tables, passing words beneath umbrellas about the true worth of each other's jewelry? We are in competition somehow, but what are the prizes?

Rayma has grabbed Milton—she has taken him aside now and I'm not even paying attention. I shout over to their bent heads, "I was supposed to decide what I want." Rayma rises before Milton, who looks somewhat shocked, drained of energy already. Rayma has a way of asking "How are you?" that tells you she already knows and thinks it's too bad. "I haven't had a chance to think about what I want," I continue. "Every time I come here I have to get my bearings again. Mom, you just arrived, you had a long flight and a taxi ride—"

And Rayma starts: "Maniac driver thinks he's in the city on these streets, nearly hit the Lenchner kid, she looks like she's grown, such a nice dress, why her mother lets her play in the street I don't know."

I try again: "So *why* don't we sit down and have some tea and maybe we can talk about what we're doing here."

"Is there tea?" Rayma asks.

"I'll check the drawers," I answer. "Sit down. Sit." Rayma uncrosses her arms and turns towards the table.

"Is there *water*?" she asks.

"I left everything on," Milton says. "Nothing has been touched."

"And so I assume you're paying for all this nothing, the electricity and this water we're not using?" Rayma faces me as she accuses my father. In the ladies' card game she's just scored a point.

"If you don't *use* it what's there to pay?" Milton says. He wipes the flat of his hand across the table before sitting down, and looks at the dust caking his palm as if at a wound, disbelieving. "Anyway I use it occasionally," he says, facing no one, facing his reflection in the wood. "It costs more to shut it off. Nothing is decided."

Rayma purses her lips at me, a small but lethal gesture. Only Milton's eyes reveal his frown.

It maddens me, this anger of my parents—so unreasonable, with no object but the vague, unanswerable frustrations of thirty years come to this. Teacups on a dark, bare table. Three coats in the foyer closet. They have widowed each other, and in their grief they rage at one another for causing such trouble. When they forget to be triumphant about the separation, they begin to put blame. It is senseless. Part of the house looks abandoned after a plague, one of those sad disasters where nothing is touched but the people, suddenly and forever. My toys, my childhood games, clothes too small or too old to wear, boxes stuffed without memory—everything abandoned ten years before is abandoned again.

And so they live in exile, and still attempt to rule. Milt stays in a furnished apartment near the downtown, with a swimming pool and a "racquet complex" (a disease, maybe; something Freud missed?) beside the gourmet restaurant. He is living on his Gulf retirement money, which he took when the company was absorbed into the larger world alongside his marriage. Rayma stays with her sister in their four-bedroom house below the main road to Snowshoe. "She's such a big skier she had to move there?" I hear still from Milton on Sunday evenings.

Am I orphaned now, or is there a real reason I should be here?

Back in my bedroom after Zeyde's funeral she told me my father lacked all initiative. I wondered if their arguments simply weren't as much fun for her anymore. I balked at everything she said. They could divorce now, she said, because Zeyde had been the last of their parents alive, the last thing keeping them together. I hadn't been a factor for years, she said.

Why does this sort of honesty always make me cringe?

"Zeyde had a good marriage," she told me. She was dry-eyed as she spoke of her father. Why I expected her to cry I don't know—an infection I caught from the movies perhaps. But I had not cried either. Zeyde had withdrawn from me years ago. He took signals from Rayma, and she thought undue attention would make me less of a man. I had mourned him then.

Zeyde was a bullet of a man, round-fleshed but compact. His whiskers would scrape my face when he kissed me at almost any time of the day, even when he still had shaving cream under each ear as he bent over the pull-out sofa on a Sunday morning and scooped up the paper that he wanted. Being quiet for Zeyde on those childhood sleepover mornings was what I sacrificed for such kisses. He was distinct from every other person in my world—even his clothes were exotic to me: sleeveless undershirts and a grey fedora with a black band and a green feather that maybe gangsters wore, and hard shoes and long pants whatever the weather.

So Rayma's marriage had been all form? And even Zeyde, never a tired man, had been defeated by his daughter. Rayma after his funeral sat on my childhood bed, on the white cover—her body barely made a dent. Before she could start to catalog Milton's various crimes a knock came at the bedroom door, and Rayma grew angry. She scowled and called "one minute" as brightly as she could. Her hands went to her face, checking her make-up, and then quickly into her black leather purse, the one with the fancy tool-work. "Hallo-o-o?" came tentatively through the closed door—her sister Myrna. Rayma pitched her head back at the door and I opened it a few inches to tell Myrna that Rayma was composing herself. I looked back. Rayma had a small white box to one eye—a long rectangle with "Las Vegas" printed on the side. It was a magnifying box with a souvenir picture I had seen many times: Zeyde's favorite trip, twenty years ago, to that town of great mystique. "Vegas," he called it. I always thought of it as "Las" myself. But he loved it, in his own way. In the picture he was younger, of course, and uncharacteristically relaxed—jacket off, shirt undone just one button. A serious man having a good, expensive time. I was ten—he brought me back a beer mug. By the time I was old enough to use it Zeyde was hardly around.

Rayma's whole face changed as she looked at the picture. For the first time in years I saw the little girl she once must have been. She was not sad over the picture—she looked like she was making a wish, concentrating, focused, on the moment and on the future. A hopeful little girl—but in a second she realized her hope was useless. She lowered the picture and let her purse fall beside her. "Myrna says the people are here with more trays," I told her. Quickly she was past me and down the hall.

My parents are finished now with their tea at the table, and waiting for me. I put the teacups in the sink.

"Rinse them out, we'll get ants," Rayma calls to the kitchen.

"So? They'll starve the next day," Milton says.

"Who's going to buy a house when they see dead ants?" Rayma says. But she does not wait for a reply. She is already halfway down the hall to the bedrooms.

My father comes up beside me and watches Rayma disappear into the darkness. "Your mother's on her own schedule," he says. "I've got to go chase her, like Ahab after that Moby Dick thing, the fish, you know." I know. I know, Milton, that when you *really* get mad at Rayma—when your back is against the wall and you're sinking into the pavement like the footprints on Hollywood Boulevard—then, Milton, then you take action.

And Rayma pushes: you, me, everyone. She pushes and she doesn't leave a mark. I often wished I could stop her from talking, Milton, when I was adult enough to realize you were stewing behind that ruddy face of yours. When I was younger, and you were still a tower seated there in your worn recliner, I would watch you when she talked to you. I have a picture in my head, Milton, a puzzling scene that means more to me now than it ever has. You're behind your newspaper, scanning, reading, as I peer at your face from the side. Always Rayma's voice calls from different parts of the house, falling and rising like an uncertain heartbeat, and with my eyes I beg you to answer her, to turn from those pages and call something happy down the hall—to still the voice, to calm her so she won't erupt later.

But you, Milton, you were even more dangerous. With Rayma we both knew what was coming—animals fled to higher ground, tribes danced in supplication, meters flipped, the radio broadcast bulletins. *You* I could never predict: there was some subtler volcanism at work. Pressure built and then you exploded, and your anger covered everything, life became stuck in the moment, and even Rayma paled.

I was in the fourth grade. The knife was only a butter knife, but when it rang against your plate and you stood with that silver in your hand I knew, and Rayma knew, that the world had changed. Rayma is human, Milton, committable perhaps, but human. You were a campsite bear, and Rayma teased and laughed at you and threw scraps through a crack in her car window. You lay about—you took the scraps—but we knew with one swipe you could break the glass and get to us.

The knife—a terrible silver. You had a voice and a size again suddenly, and merely standing forced Rayma back into the kitchen. You followed. I watched the whole thing from your brown recliner, standing beside it as I seem to be doing in all my childhood memories.

It happened very quickly. Nothing is like that today. The days are heavy now: chew on them, they grow fatter. With the knife you were in the kitchen and shouting at Rayma before I knew you'd risen. Backing, Rayma's head pushed the flowered kitchen curtains aside and bumped the window, making silhouettes of you both in the sun. You shouted and the sound was worse than the knife, held motionless in the air like a stick. Noise from the quiet man, so terrifying.

I don't remember your words—Rayma only answered for a while. I finally noticed my own trembling when you slowed down and talked to her, your head dipping slowly as you made your points. Then it was quiet. Your dark shape was motionless. Then you bent to kiss her forehead, and turned away.

Tell me, Milton, what made you stop?

I've lost them, where are my parents? Muffled voices from a bedroom, agitated. Great noises of destruction. They are emptying a closet. I feel like I've got a pair of two-year-olds to watch when I let them go for a minute.

Rayma has the contents of my closet spread across the bedroom floor. She's on her knees in front of it, her suit pulling tight as she disappears for another bundle. I watch from the doorway. While Rayma lifts a bag out of the closet Milton examines a previous find. Rayma has to pause and watch him over her shoulder each time. "You don't want that," she says again and again. "What do you want that for? Throw it out." Milton has a small pile beside him, Rayma nothing. She packed away my childhood years ago, knows the contents of each box at a glance. She isn't even looking inside anything, but she is still digging. The suitcases she brought are for her own clothes, the ones remaining in her closet.

"Do you see this, Willy?" Milton holds up a worn wallet embossed with the Boy Scout emblem. When we used to tour historic sites on vacation he had the same expression on his face—discoverer and inventor at once. "Do you remember that camp, Willy?" he says. But he discards the wallet to look in another box.

Rayma is finished. Several bags remain in the middle of the closet floor—she has moved them around but left them untouched. She rises with surprising energy. "Move the bed for me, Willy," she says. "Make sure there's nothing under it." My old bed is as light as the shell of an insect left on a tree. Nothing but dust tumbleweeds in that dark canyon. Rayma peers hard, frowns. "You take what you want," she tells me, motioning toward the closet. I'll never look at any of this, but I don't want her to throw these artifacts out. Milton is digging deeper in the clutter. "Zeyde's watch," he says quietly, and pulls out a pocketwatch without cover or hands. The dial is an old creamy white, waterstained, with Roman numerals strung round the edges like high tide marks. Zeyde gave that to me when I was very young, to aid my grown-up fantasies. Rayma steps past both of us and heads towards her bedroom.

"Stay here a minute," Milton says to me. "I'm through chasing her." He shoves his pile of momentos aside and pats the rug. I let myself sink beside him cross-legged.

"I don't know what's going to go on here, Willy—whether your mother and I are ever really going to see eye to eye on this thing, or whether we're just going to keep splitting our lives up till we start ripping each other out of the goddamn photo albums to get some peace. I feel very selfish, Willy. I mean this has nothing to do with you." I nod at my father. It wouldn't do to try to explain in my own words what he means, to signal through translation that I'm sure I under-stand. He would simply repeat his original words and wait for the nod. "This is a simple solution, Willy. A little crazy, maybe, but simple. I eat better—before, Willy, everything had begun to stick in my gut, you know what I mean? I feel better. It's all over." Milton palms up Zeyde's watch and hands it to me. "Just do me a favor, Willy, okay? You want to do me a favor? Don't blame her. Just don't blame her for this."

I drop the watch in my pocket and get to my feet. Milton is calm, breathing easily—he is made of clay, a red-faced idol, a model of nirvana, broken and healed. I am depressed. I am stupefied. Where is his anger? Doesn't he owe it to himself to be angry? Doesn't he owe it to me?

The hall is dark—Rayma has only a small lamp lit in her bedroom. She's got purses from seven centuries spread across the bare kingsize mattress. I stop in the doorway. She is absorbed in sorting—she is tossing purses aside as if she were in a struggle to win something—Macy's biggest bargain sale. Suddenly she alights on a flashy find—her black bag, with the leather fancywork. She checks it over, the zippers, the snaps and flaps and secret pockets. Searching for coins?

Not our Rayma. The search is proving futile—she starts her rounds again. I bang the side of the doorway and she notices me.

"Do you want any of *these?*" she asks me, laughing at herself and the scene. I manage a smile. Rayma looked so innocent there searching a moment ago that I almost wanted to help her. She pushes the purses aside and draws the leather bag down into her lap, hugging it to herself. She is a child all of a sudden, treasuring the first signs of womanhood. I am happy for her.

Zeyde's watch is light in my pocket. It bumps against another object, an oblong white box, a souvenir of sunny, ancient Las Vegas. It is something I've carried with me since Zeyde's funeral. But I don't give it back to Rayma. She is on her own.

RENÉE MANFREDI

Driving with Mimi

"YOUR GRANDMOTHER FELL out of the sink this morning," was what my mother called New York to tell me. I asked what Mimi was doing in the sink and Janice, my mother, said, "Who knows? But she hit her head against the stove and had to have four stitches. This is the beginning of the end."

Janice had been predicting "the end," by which she meant the decline in Mimi's health and mental acuity, since divorcing my father and moving to Ann Arbor ten years ago. She wanted Mimi to sell her house and land in Tennessee and join her in Michigan. Mimi always refused, said, "I've raised eight children and a husband, and by God this is the first time in my life that I can reheat leftovers in the same containers I store them in."

Janice's informant was Carlton Tripp. He lived exactly two dirt roads and a cow pasture from Mimi and was her closest neighbor. It was Carlton who had reported Mimi's sink tumble and took her to the hospital to be stitched.

"This just nettles the peace out of me," Janice had said. "My own mother living way out there in East Jesus, near to nothing and no one if she really needs anything. Carlton said last week he watched as she put her groceries away, and she put the bath soap in the refrigerator and the oranges on the shower caddy next to the shampoo. This is one of the earliest signs of senility."

"Or grief," I said. Mimi's best friend, Ernest Dean Vaughn, had died about a year ago. Ernest Dean had never married and when Mimi became widowed it was Ernest who "rekindled her interest in life's particulars again," as she put it.

"I don't see why you can't go out and attend to her," Janice said. Actually, I didn't either. I'd come to New York with no nameable business except escape. I was twenty-five, a college dropout for the third time, and had just broken up with with my fiancée, Neil, a marine biology major as I was. But unlike me, he was a proficient diver and entirely at ease with depth.

I thought there would be certain signs in a place the size of Manhattan, something that would signal what I should do next. The life you envy is the life that should be yours, someone once said, but I hadn't even *met* anybody except my roommate, a manic-depressive, would-be actress from Weehawken who in one euphoric afternoon painted all of our walls lilac.

So, I left for Mimi's at the beginning of April. Janice had arranged it all, and Carlton Tripp picked me up at the bus station in his '57 Chevy convertible with the top permanently stuck down. The air carried the scent of earth newly tilled. Beyond the fields, the mountains still had winter on them, wrinkled and powdered with snow like sugared figs.

"Now, I expect I should warn you your grandma has been doing things not in keeping with her usual patterns," Carlton said as we pulled up to Mimi's.

I looked at him. "So my mother tells me." I'd known Carlton Tripp since I was a little girl. He was a kind of local tragedy. Within the space of a year, his wife ran off with a meat inspector, his cows stopped yielding and he lost all of his teeth and his sense of humor. He now wore a look of composed dissatisfaction.

Mimi was in the kitchen, on her hands and knees sanding the baseboards. An old phonograph in the center of the room played Glenn Miller's "In the Mood." Mimi sanded to the beat. The room was flooded with sun and the air was thick with the scent of pears.

"Mimi," Carlton shouted. He lifted the needle from the record. "Mimi, your granddaughter is here."

She stood, walked over to me and squinted.

"I'm Valerie," I said, thinking she might not recognize me or known I was coming.

"Well of course you are," she said. "I was just noticing your cheaters. When did you take to wearing them so thick?" She pulled off my eyeglasses and pinched the lens between her thumb and forefinger. "You're awfully short-sighted." She handed them back to me. "Well. Your mother reports that you're shiftless and lacking in ambition."

"I'll just be going now," Carlton said.

"Goodbye," Mimi said.

"If you need anything, Mimi—"

"Goodbye, goodbye, and happy trails to you!"

I thanked Carlton for the ride and then he left.

"Ha! There's a man who thinks solitude's just another name for sorrow. Always skulking about. Can't say that I trust a man whose name backwards is a bully's taunt. *Tripp Carlton.*" She giggled. "Well? Why are you here, and how long are you staying?"

I shrugged. "I just needed some time to figure things out." She narrowed her eyes, drew her mouth up.

"And my apartment in Manhattan has bugs."

"Oh, all right. When you're ready to leave remind me to give you some boric acid. It'll kill everything that draws breath."

Because of her arthritis, Mimi kept the thermostat set at

seventy-five. My bedroom was on the third floor and seemed to pool all of the heat. I awakened in the middle of the night feeling a weight bearing down, my lungs stuffed with air. Opening the windows made it worse since the cool night wind just made the radiators pour out more heat, the kicking and clanking of it through the ducts sounding like a penned mule flailing its hooves against a tin bucket. So I began sleeping on the roof. After the first few nights I learned where the declivities were, exactly how to position myself so I wouldn't awaken in the morning with my ankle wedged against the gutter spout.

"What in the sweet name of Jesus are you doing?" Mimi had shouted (*shouted*) up to me the first morning. She was up on the ladder putting out seed in the bird house hung from an elm. I explained about the temperature and she found endless amusement in it. I'd come downstairs in the morning, for instance, my cheek imprinted with seams and squares from the roof's irregularities, and she would point in mock horror, say, "You've got shingles!" Or, "You didn't fall off the roof, did you?" which was supposedly a euphemism for menstruation.

Mimi's own bedroom was on the first floor and had been a screened-in porch at one time. It was the coldest room in the house despite getting the full morning sun. The windows were poorly caulked and didn't prevent drafts from gathering when the wind was high. Only her arthritis and the stairs kept her from trading rooms with me, she said, but I came to enjoy it out there, outside the stuffy bedroom with its heat and its history: it had been my mother's girlhood bedroom and before that Mimi's own. Inside the closet door were their height charts, initials and ages beside two columns of chalk marks. Against the dark paint they looked like spinal X-rays, each vertebra visible. Janice's chart ended when she reached nineteen, the date of her marriage beside a thick, final line. Mimi's went on impossibly until aged thirty, though she had reached her full height at sixteen, was as tall as I was now at twenty-five. And, too, by my age she was already married for nine years, the babies coming every other year, regular as the tide.

But if sleeping outside meant escaping the heat, in its place was something almost as bad: insects. Tiny spiders. An occasional moth, fireflies that brushed against my face. It was precisely this onslaught of living things coming at me in the dark that allowed Neil and me to go from being lab partners to lovers. I insisted that he wrap his body around mine when we jumped into the water, not let go until we reached twenty feet. Sometimes he held me the whole way down and things just went on from there.

The first fifteen feet or so of a dive was what we called "night-blind," the initial immersion where you're speeding downward before your eyes have time to adjust to the change in light and anything that touches you—algae, starfish, somebody's knee—feels large and dangerous. "It's a leap of faith," Neil said, but I never could learn to trust the dark. And the awful gurgling the water makes when its surface is broken, something I imagined would come from the drowning. As soon as I could look up and see the sun shallows jagging through the waves I'd be fine. I even learned to enjoy the way everything seemed to be in pantomime the deeper we went. "You have to get over these fears, Valerie," Neil had said. "There isn't always going to be somebody to guide you to the deep."

"I know that. But maybe I want to study life in shallow water."

I read somewhere that Galileo, going a little mad in his later years, carried in his palm at all times a mirror the size of a silver dollar. Supposedly, what he couldn't bear was the vastness of the galaxy and this was a way for him to have a piece of the sky any time he opened his hand. One night I dreamed that I found Galileo's mirror. It was in an underwater cave, but in the center was a reflection of Venus. The more I reached for it, the faster it sped downward, until I was at the bottom of the ocean with no oxygen left in my tank.

I went downstairs to find Mimi. She was in her bedroom

painting her nails crimson. She looked up at me. "What are you doing up at this God-forsaken hour?"

"I had a dream." She pointed to the bed. I sat. "Mimi, how do you know if you're in love? What if you think you're in love, but you only feel tender toward somebody during one activity?"

She looked at me over the top of her bifocals. "You mean sex, I understand."

"No, actually I mean deep-sea diving."

The corners of her mouth drew up. "Well, if you only love somebody while fully immersed, I'd say the union is all washed up."

"Mimi, please, this is serious."

"Ha! At your age nothing should be serious." She let a few minutes go by. "Well, do you feel a kind of ache when you're not with him? Like your flesh feels heavy and draped around a void?"

I shook my head.

"Well, when you're with him, do you feel a kind of warmth bubbling up from here?" She touched the place just below her breastbone.

"No, I don't feel that, either."

"Then what *do* you feel?"

"I don't know. Maybe kind of thirsty."

"Well. It may be love, it may be diabetes." She waved her hands to dry the nailpolish, then leaned forward suddenly, jabbed a finger at me. "Don't marry anybody unless you feel that if you can't spend the rest of your life with him you will die. I myself wanted to wait for five or six years before I married. I could have had just half of my children and that would have been plenty."

"What would you have done with those six years?"

"Lived! I would have honored all of my urges. Guiltlessly."

Neil's marriage proposal came about as a kind of fluke, a pure coincidence that can happen only in natural phenomena. We had just seen a shark. It circled us for about fifteen minutes, coming so close that I could see the veins threaded through the fins. Neil took my hand and we didn't move. And when it went away I felt the exhilaration that rushes in after fear. Neil slid his hand from mine and eased down the hood of my wet suit, freeing my hair until it floated in tendrils.

On a lichen-covered rock in a shallower part of the water, we made love among the coral. Afterwards, he traced the words, "Marry me" in the sand with a shard of stone. I nodded my head yes, but after that day we never discussed marriage again. Later, to try to evoke the feeling, Neil bought a sound machine that was supposed to be white noise. It had three tracks: waves crashing against the shore, the low hum of a motor and distant traffic. We made love to all three but I didn't feel anything except distracted, especially during the track of a humming motor.

Mimi held her hands out in front of me. "That's what I call an eye-getting shade. It's called 'Winter Poppies.' "

"Magnetic," I said.

She tilted her glasses up with the heels of her hands and peered closely at me. "You could be a real stunner, you know that? If you did something with your hair and got rid of those cheaters. Have you tried wearing those disks that go directly in your eyes?"

"Contact lenses? I tried them for a while but they never felt right. I was always afraid of losing them."

"A woman is at the height of her beauty in her twenties. With exceptions, of course. I myself retained my full flower into my forties. My own mother turned heads at sixty."

Mimi *was* beautiful at forty; one Thanksgiving day I slipped away from the throng of family and found boxes of photographs in her attic. There were hundreds of pictures of her. There was also quite a few of Mimi and my grandfather at his company picnic. But instead of sitting next to her husband, she was almost always beside a tall man with green eyes and hair so dark it seemed to shed light. Mimi, next to him, looked so vibrant and alive that I'd imagined it was her expression itself which had kept the photographs from yellowing.

Mimi leaned forward now, took a strand of my hair between her fingers. "Do you use a rinse?"

"I have been. Believe it or not, I've found grey already."

"Is it a peroxide?"

"Semi-permanent. It washes out in about six shampoos."

"Oh, well, you have to be careful."

"With hair dye?"

"With things that are semi-permanent."

I awoke the next morning to a weak sun and a light rain. There was a strong scent of earth. From inside the house I heard Mimi's music blaring, The Ink Spots' "I Don't Want To Set the World on Fire."

I pulled my blankets inside, out of the rain and sat straddling the window sill, one leg against the (hot) radiator, one stretched out on the roof. The air was very cool, stirring, as though a storm might be inching up. I looked up at the sky, tried to spot any morning stars; Jupiter was supposed to be aspected early in the day this time of year. Before I left for New York, Neil and I had begun to visit the planetarium. We always got high first, then went to their mid-afternoon star show. He had a habit of quoting philosophers as soon as they dimmed the lights. One time he turned to me and whispered. "Man lives in the abyss between the infinitely large and the infinitely small. Pascal said that." The simulated stars raced above us and were reflected in Neil's glasses.

"Really? Was that before or after he learned to pasteurize milk?" I hated it when he felt compelled to comment on mystery.

Just past the garden, I noticed now, were footprints heading out to the road that led to Carlton Tripp's or to nowhere, depending on how far you went. When the rain started to pelt I closed the window and went downstairs to find Mimi.

She was in the kitchen standing at the window above the sink and not moving. The table was set for two with the good china and stemware. "Mimi," I said, and she turned and gave me a cautious, hostile look. Her hair was perfectly styled and she was wearing makeup. "What are you doing?"

She stared at me as though trying to match my face with my voice. "I suppose I'm waiting."

"For what?" I said.

She fussed at the stove, paced from the table back to the window. "I don't know what to do, how to get them."

"Get who, Mimi?"

"Not who, *them*. I wanted a nice dinner, so I'm cooking chicken. But you have to have breakfast before you can have dinner, and I can't cook any eggs."

"We have eggs, we have lots of eggs," I said and walked to the refrigerator.

"No, no, in here," she said, pulling me down to look into the oven. There was a frozen chicken on the rack.

"I didn't plan ahead. Now here's the hen and there's not much she can yield frozen and dead."

At first I thought she was joking, but her expression was a child-like amazement creased with an old woman's confusion. For the first time I could imagine her putting tangerines next to the shampoo and toothpaste in the vegetable crisper.

It was then I looked down and noticed her legs. Her pantyhose were torn in gashes, her skin cut and bleeding. "Mimi, what happened? what happened to your legs?" Her shoes were thick with mud and there were burrs stuck to the hem of her dress.

"I went for a walk. Is that so terrible? Can't I even go for a walk without you following me?"

"I'm going to make you some tea." I led her into the living room and eased her into the chair by the window.

What I saw next was just my eyes playing tricks on me, but as I was carrying the tray with the tea, the steam rose up and clouded my glasses. When I looked at Mimi, the white of her hair blended with the fog on my lenses and it appeared as though I were seeing her naked skull, articulate and smooth against the festive pink of the afghan wrapped around her.

I spilled the sugar.

She turned and her face came back into my focus.

"Where were you today, Mimi?" I sat in front of her, pressed a cloth to the cuts on her legs. She was taking blood thinner medication and consequently coagulation was slow; her body seemed determined to shed every last platelet.

"Yes, indeed, this is some weather. This is a chunk-floating rain if ever I witnessed."

A silence slid down.

"Sometimes," she said softly, "I'm afraid of what the weather might do to me."

"The rain is outside, it can't hurt you."

She flattened her hand against the window as if to confirm this. "But do you suppose the weather can change what you know and remember?"

"No, I don't think so."

"Well, *I* do. I think the lightning that happens in the sky can happen inside your head. It can make time skip the track."

"What do you mean?"

"That one minute I'm waiting for Ernest Dean to come to dinner, and in the next instant I feel something inside me bunch up and then I'm someplace else, watching him die. Or maybe the lightning can make you see what you *would* be remembering if the life you really wanted had been yours."

"Why do you think the weather has anything to do with regret?"

She looked at me, her face blank. "I don't know. But certain people are kin to storms. Important things happen to them when it rains. I'm going to die during weather like this."

"Don't say that, Mimi. You have a lot of life yet."

"Your mother thinks I'm too old to have my wits."

"Well, I don't think so. I think you have all of your wits. Probably more than your share."

"Your mother says I'm senile."

"You're not."

She looked at me closely, as though to make sure I really believed it.

"Do you think there's such a thing that exists?"

"Senility? I guess so."

She looked away, up at the sky. "Just after Ernest Dean died, I dreamed of this wheel of light, circles around a black space. I knew the lights to be my years, and I saw myself moving around them. But when I reached the last one, I found I was just one circle away from where I began. I had to choose between falling through the darkness or starting all over again."

"Which did you choose?"

"To fall. Maybe being senile just means refusing to relive your memories but having nothing to take their place."

For three days, during which it rained without pause, Mimi took to her bed, convinced she had a collapsed lung. She made me promise not to call the doctor. I said, "If you're in pain, don't you think a doctor might be able to help?"

"I'm not in pain," she said. "It only feels like there's a deflated balloon impaled on one of my ribs."

"And that's not painful?"

Her face was flushed and her eyes had a fevered brightness. She looked positively *giddy*, though from what I couldn't say.

"Isn't it peculiar?" she murmured, looking up at the ceiling.

"What?" I said.

"That something has to collapse before you learn how light the body really is. There's this weight on one side of me, but the healthy lung feels feathery as soap bubbles."

"I'm calling the doctor," I said.

She grabbed by wrist. "Don't. There's no pain. It just feels like indigestion. Like what you feel when you wake up from a bad sleep. It's an undigested darkness, is all."

I considered calling my mother in Ann Arbor, but I was afraid she'd catch the next plane to Tennessee, drag along a priest and talk Mimi into dying. So I moved in a cot and slept in Mimi's room, which, because of the relative coolness and all of the windows, was the next best thing to sleeping outside. Except that in here I was closer to the earth than I was to the sky.

One night something startled me out of a deep sleep. I sat up, tried to figure out what it was that awakened me. I didn't hear anything. *Nothing.* The silence was as palpable as the cold air. I looked over at Mimi. She was very still. I touched her, whispered her name, but she didn't move.

On the night table was her compact, and I opened it, held the mirror beneath her nostrils, but the room was so dark that I couldn't see anything on it when I brought it away. Then I remembered her rosary beads. In a cloth box on her bureau I knew she kept a rosary that glowed in the dark. I went over and got it out, stretched out the beads on the floor between our beds.

I held my eyeglasses beneath Mimi's nose for a few moments, then quickly put them on and stared down at the glowing green globes on the floor: they were blurry, haloed, then slowly came into sharp focus as her breath evaporated. I repeated this, just to be sure.

"What are you doing?" Her voice was sharp, piercing.

"I thought you might be dead."

"Well, think again." And after a pause she said, "The rain has stopped for now. I would like to be by myself."

I looked over at the window. The rain was gone; I hadn't noticed until just that moment.

"Okay. I'll leave you. If you need anything, Mimi—"

"Goodnight, goodnight and magic dreams to you," she said.

I went upstairs, dried off the roof and didn't wake up until I felt the sun on my eyelids.

The sky was mottled this morning, patches of grey and blue ribboned through white as though the collision of clouds in the dark had left bruises. The air was cool and still damp, but nevertheless I felt the onslaught of spring, smelled crocuses, heard the lyrical delirium of crows and wood thrushes calling across the fields, just past the row of chinaberry trees.

It was for this reason, this sense of well-being and calm that comes at the genesis of a season, that I did not go to check immediately on Mimi as I would have in inclement weather. And anyway, when I went back inside to dress I heard Mimi's radio playing from downstairs. It was Saturday morning and she always listened to a station that played reruns of shows like "Fibber McGee and Molly" or "The Shadow."

I rummaged through my closet, took my time dressing, enjoyed the way the air felt on my body. Back in New York I wore a uniform when I waitressed and it had been a long time since I had been in anything other than stained polyester or jeans. So I chose a fuchsia cotton pullover and a linen floral skirt that came nearly to my ankles, irises and cabbage roses blooming down the length of me.

I went downstairs to find Mimi, tell her I was going to take her to lunch to celebrate spring. The radio was playing in her bedroom but she wasn't there. I checked the kitchen. Then outside: nowhere.

I sat by the window to wait. It was still early and the day was bright, marred only by a few dark clouds that didn't look as though they held rain.

But by ten o'clock the light was noticeably more muted and I decided to walk over to Carlton Tripp's to see if he might know where Mimi was.

He was sitting on the porch when I got there, staring into space the way some people stare at the ocean, with a look of expectation and dread.

"Carlton," I said. "Mimi's missing. I suspect she's gone to the cemetery where Ernest Dean Vaughn is buried."

His eyes traveled down the length of me then upward, to the sky.

"That might very well be. She visits a lot."

From the TV inside the house I heard Jackie Gleason's laughter on a rerun of "The Honeymooners." Saturdays in this town set the media back about forty years.

"Well, how do I get there?"

"It's a good three miles," he said looking down at my shoes. "You're welcome to take old Beatrice," he said, gesturing toward his car. "I'd drive you myself but I'm expecting company. Course you no doubt remember that she's a convertible who long ceased to convert. She just keeps her top stuck down."

He followed close behind me to the driveway. "You better hurry if you want to race the rain. A fair sky this time of year don't last but half a day."

He gave me directions, leaned his elbows in the window when I started the engine. He squinted at me then said, "What time's the party?"

"What party?"

"The one you're plainly havin' or guesting at. A woman don't dress herself up like that to fetch her grandmother from a cemetery."

I pulled out onto the road, repeating the directions over in my head: straight; left at the half-burned barn; straight again past the gas station; turn right into cemetery, entrance unmarked so pay attention, and once inside look for statue of crouched lion. The lion was the plot vicinity of Ernest Dean's grave.

It began to drizzle when I reached the half-burned barn and by the time I turned into the cemetery, not only was the rain coming down fiercely, the dense foliage and pines blocked out almost all of the light. It was as though I'd gone straight from afternoon into midnight.

The rain streaked down my glasses and the road ahead seemed to ripple.

Straight ahead in the yellow haze of my high beams, I saw what looked to be the lion. I stopped the car and walked over to it, but it turned out to to be just a configuration of stones.

I followed a footpath where the underbrush and tree branches on either side of me jagged against my ankles, my face.

I was lost. One headstone looked like another, each path identical to the one I just left. I stood still and shouted Mimi's name. The rain hitting against a small spade abandoned near a grave marker made a cold, tinny music.

The rain can't hurt you, was what went through my head as I kept walking. And then the stern reprimand one of my biology professors gave me when he saw the unusual way Neil and I began each dive: "A fear of water is not a natural one, Miss Sparr. We, after all, begin life in water. We carry it in our bodies. A fear of water is nothing more than a veiled fear of life."

When I found Mimi I almost fell over her. She was huddled in her white rain cape, arms around the headstone as though it were keeping her afloat. And here was the lion, its cement mouth frozen open in the middle of warning or protest, drooling rain.

"Mimi." I bent down, touched her.

"My God!" she said. "You scared me."

"Didn't you hear me calling you?"

She nodded.

"Then why didn't you answer?"

"I didn't recognize your voice. And I can't be answering to everything that calls my name."

"Mimi, we should be going now. I have Carlton Tripp's car."

"I'd like to wait just a little while longer," she said, and ran her fingers over the letters carved in the headstone.

"Wait for what?"

"This," she said, pulling a small, framed photograph out of her pocket, "was myself and Ernest Dean. I was twenty-two, six years into marriage, Ernest Dean was thirty, six years into a long wait."

It was a studio portrait, Mimi and Ernest Dean posed side by side, Ernest Dean with one of her hands between both of his, half-raised, as though the minute the photograph was snapped he pressed it to his lips. Mimi herself looked straight into the camera with a look that seemed composed in equal parts of joy and defiance. "We have stolen this time together," her look seemed to say, "for love. *So there.*"

"Look at the strength of his jaw," she said, tracing it with the edge of her crimson-painted fingernail. "He had the most remarkable hands. He could take away my headaches by just pressing here and there."

I tilted the photograph up to angle it away from the glare. "He *was* handsome."

"Ha! Handsome is not the word. There was so much to him you had to look at him twice just to take him all in."

I handed the photograph back to her, said, "We need to be going. Carlton's car must be filled with water by now."

"I want to wait."

"For what?"

"For Ernest. Today might be the day Ernest Dean and I are reunited."

"Mimi, Ernest is dead. You're touching his grave right now." My voice sounded hollow, flat.

"I know that. You think I don't know that the only man I ever loved is right here? He died on a day just like this. As I will. The weather will reunite us. I loved this man."

"I know."

"No you don't. You don't know what love is. You don't know how it feels until it turns into something you have to fight for." She looked away from me. "I was just fifteen when we met. I used to climb down the rose trellis at midnight to be with him. Daddy found us out and sent me to St. Louis for a year to live with his sister. When I came back is when he forced me to marry your granddaddy. Said I was lucky any man would want me, spoiled as I was. Said I'd rot like some fruit that'd been split open and its stone plucked away. And when my husband died and Ernest could reclaim me, your mother and that meddler Carlton Tripp jump to suspicions. The eight years I had with Ernest Dean were the only truly happy ones in my life."

She raked the earth with her fingers, digging down deep. A few minutes slipped by. "I think the rain is letting up a little," I said.

"You think so?" She looked up at the sky. "It still feels angry to me."

"But it's not as cold. The rain isn't as cold as it was, do you think?"

"Yes, it *does* feel like it's falling from clouds closer to the sun."

"I think that means it will stop soon," I said.

"Okay," she said, and didn't resist when I helped her stand. She seemed so tiny, so fragile inside that cape. "I'm not hurting you, am I, Mimi?" I said and helped her find her footing.

"I'm made of scrap iron," she said.

Carlton Tripp's car had at least two inches of water on the floor and seat. Mimi giggled. She sat in the water without flinching. "Puddles!"

I couldn't see much beyond the path of the headlights and I drove slowly. (Crawled). Mimi rested her head back and seemed unperturbed by the rain hitting her upturned face.

I stopped the car in the middle of the road. "Mimi, I can't see anything."

She looked in front and behind us. "I can't either. Just plunge ahead on faith." When we got to the road that led to Carlton Tripp's, she touched my arm, said, "Not just yet. I don't want to go home just yet. Keep driving."

"Where to?"

"No where-to. Just drive."

I followed the road we were on, past Carlton Tripp's, past Mimi's house.

I tilted the side view mirror up so I could look at the sky. The rain eased up a little, but not enough to improve visibility. Out of the corner of my eye I saw Mimi arranging her hair. It was flattened close to her head from being wet and her scalp peeked through. "I had such a head of hair when I was younger," she said. "Ernest Dean liked to shampoo and comb it. In my later years, I mean."

"Did Granddaddy know you loved Ernest Dean?"

"When we married he knew what had gone on before. But he and Ernest Dean worked for the same company and I always sat with Ernest Dean at the picnics and such."

"Did he get mad?"

"Gave me a couple of good boar-hoggings, is all."

"What's that?"

She looked over at me. "I believe it's what you young people today call a revenge fuck."

I laughed, felt her watching me.

"I take back what I thought about you earlier," she said.

"What was that?"

"That you're mealy-mouthed and ungrateful."

"Oh. Thanks, I guess." I was driving almost on the shoulder of the road now, afraid a car would come in the opposite direction and sideswipe me.

"When I was your age, I would have sold part of my future to have the choices you have. You can study life underwater if you want. You can marry whoever you choose whenever you want. You can get divorced if you make a mistake."

"Except that I'm twenty-five and still don't know what I want. But, anyway, why did you change your mind?"

"I think the only problem you have is you haven't learned to let go."

"Let go of what?"

"Turn right, here. This will take us to the highway."

I turned. This road was smooth, paved. I checked the rear view mirror. The sky was beginning to break, freckle with color.

"Don't worry about what's behind you. This road is one-way. Ernest Dean and I used to have grand fun along this stretch. Speeding has always been my one true vice. Course Ernest Dean and I were usually snot-slinging drunk. A little faster, dear."

I watched as the speedometer climbed from forty to forty-five, then fifty.

"Faster."

I pressed the accelerator to the floor. The car seemed to take the road so smoothly that I wondered if I was hydro-planing. The wind dried the rain on my glasses.

Mimi held onto the dashboard. "Soon you'll merge into the highway, but don't worry about yielding. Just honor your speed."

She glanced behind us. "There's nothing coming. Commit to seventy and merge."

I held my breath and aimed.

"Good." Mimi laughed above the wind. "You're doing fine."

I relaxed my hands on the wheel, let some slackness back into my leg muscles. "There's nothing to this," was what I turned to Mimi to say, but just then a truck with its high beams on approached in the opposite direction. I looked away, but the light slowly arched around and blinded me. My foot slipped off the pedal. I swerved a little to the right, grazed the guardrail.

"Don't be afraid," Mimi said, and for an instant the light was something I could almost feel: a warmth pooling all around as we moved back out into the dark, speeding.

LINDA MILLER

Watching for Coyotes

COREY LIVED WITH chickens. She'd been living with them for twenty-two years, and she'd be living with them for at least twenty-two more. Or so she figured. She'd been seeing the day-olds come onto the farm in trucks packed in cardboard crates, one on top of the other—forty thousand now for their two houses. She'd lift off the serrated cover and pour out the mound of yellow fur like cream, soft and thick. Then she'd wait and watch them grow—six weeks most likely, give or take a few. Then they'd be loaded up on a truck, sometimes on the same one they came in on, and shipped off to market. She'd clean up the houses then, hosing down the cedar chips and droppings. That would take about two weeks tops. And it would start all over again. She never minded it, the routine. She was a chicken farmer. That's what she was supposed to do.

Her father was a chicken farmer working with her out in the houses. She'd been thinking about that since the day-olds came and he got ill. The doctor told him to stay in bed. He'd lay there and hack up brown phlegm, then spit it into a spittoon. He didn't think anything of it, said the spit reminded him of the tobacco he used to chew. He'd hold a wad in his mouth and his cheek would bulge out, making the lines in his skin pull smooth. His cracks would show up like the fine footprints the chicks leave behind. She liked looking at them and wondering where they led, but he'd turn his head aside, blow the wad out and make his cheeks sink under his eyes. He'd look back then, down into his magazine, and the lines on his face weren't those of day-olds anymore. No. They were three-weekers and four-, claw marks of chickens searching for feed, beaks poking into the ground, beat after beat, sharp. Yet now when she looked at him, easing back into the pillow after the spitting, the cracks weren't the same. They didn't look like any she'd ever seen before.

"Need anything?" She rested her hand on his shoulder, on the cotton of his red long johns.

He coughed and shook his head back and forth, pressing down the bulges of the pillow with each turn. His head looked so long and narrow up against the goose down. His nose pointed out, twisting slightly at the tip. It made a shadow on his lips—lips that were thin and parched. She pulled the quilt up to his shoulders.

"Any sick?" he asked.

She shook her head. "Doing fine. They'll get their feathers soon."

He nodded. "Handling it all right, are you?" He coughed again. "Haven't seen any coyotes?"

"No. Everything's fine."

"I'll be up soon. Just you watch." He rolled over then, and pulled the covers around his shoulders.

Corey closed the door to his room and headed down the stairs. She pulled on a sweater hanging from a coat tree in the hall, then pushed open the screen door and stepped outside. The chicken houses stood side by side near the road. Only the air vents jutting out from the walls interrupted the line of fiberglass—two rectangles surrounded by wide open fields. She followed the driveway, kicking up dirt with her boots; it led to the road, swinging by the coops, around them and out of sight.

The ground had turned brown, waiting for the first snowfall. Corey hoped the temperature would drop and keep the soil solid. It wasn't good for the chicks dragging mud inside. They might catch some disease, spread it through the whole flock within days and kill thousands. She'd be up nights then, prowling through the houses, picking up dead birds and burning them in the incinerator behind the coops. She shivered, hugged her arms around her chest and tried to keep the cold from whipping through the weave of her cardigan.

She slipped into the side alcove, pulled off her sweater and hung it on a hook on the wall. She stepped into a pan of disinfectant and cleaned off her boots, then opened the door into the coop. The chicks moved towards her steps, clamoring at her ankles. They clumped together like one solid mass of cotton unable to separate, chirping in unison. She waded through them, careful not to step on any, straight to the feeder that lined the floor and moved grain throughout the coop. They followed her, crawling on top of each other, making soft mounds. Corey leaned down and pulled them off one another. They'll learn to be afraid of sound in a day or two, she thought, but it still frightened her that they wanted to follow her—follow her everywhere. She checked the level of food flowing through the feeder. It was right. Then she swam back through the birds to the door and closed it behind her.

"Hey there."

Corey turned around. Lance was on top of his pinto, swinging the reins around in his hand.

"What you doing, Corinda?"

"What you doing, Lance?"

She hated being called Corinda even though that was her real name. And she never really thought of herself as anything but Corey anyway. Her mother was a Melinda—

Melinda Coriander Gibb. She never knew her. She died when Corey was a few days old. Corey wasn't even Corey then. Her mother was way too sick for anyone to bother naming her right then and there. So they waited—waited until Melinda died so that her father felt he should name the daughter after her. So Melinda Coriander became a Corinda Gibb. Later he told her that Melinda Coriander wasn't a name fit for a chicken farmer. But Corinda—now that's a name for you. Perfect. Corey never felt like a Corinda, though, refusing to pronounce all those difficult syllables from the time she could talk. She was always a Corey, plain and simple.

"I'm calling on you, Corinda Gibb."

"No one calls on Corinda."

"I do."

"That's your mistake, Lance."

"Ah, Corinda." He slipped off his horse and walked towards her. "How's the load?"

"Doing fine. Only lost a few." She kept heading towards the chicken houses.

"You shipping them out soon?" He moved up next to her and put his hand on her elbow. Corey stopped.

"Not for three weeks. You want to help out?"

He shrugged. "You want to go for a ride?"

"I don't have any time."

"Got to check on those birds?" He cupped his other hand around her elbow and looked straight into her eyes. "How about going out tonight? Nothing wrong with leaving those birds at night, is there?"

"No."

"Is that a yes?"

"I don't know." She never knew about Lance—always following her around. She thought if she was quiet enough maybe he wouldn't stick near her. Then at times it was the opposite. And she was hopping around him like a newborn with a piece of shell sticking to her. She turned and slipped her arm from his grip, then glanced sideways at him, cocking her head. She smiled. "Maybe I'll go with you. But not long. My father's ill."

Lance squeezed her arm. "I'll be by around seven." He patted her one more time then turned, walked over to his horse and hitched up into the saddle.

Corey stood underneath the horse. Her dark hair was tied back in a braid exposing her face: brown eyes, high cheekbones that curved down towards her nose, white cheeks speckled red from the wind, and thin lips. Her jacket hung over her shoulder and the sleeves covered her hands. She dug her boot into the ground.

"Wear something special," he said. Then he pulled the reins against the horse's neck and headed down the driveway.

She watched him disappear behind the coops. Mud splashed up from the horse's hooves. She turned towards the chicken houses, walked a few steps, stopped, then turned back and headed home.

She pulled open the door to her closet and shuffled through the dresses and skirts on hangers. Greys, blacks, and whites flipped past her, mostly cotton. But there wasn't one special thing—nothing. It wasn't like she never had been out on a date, she thought. She went dancing up at Caruther's Bar with Bobby Hathaway just two summers ago. She didn't have a very good time, with Bobby pawing her and his bad breath. She kept excusing herself to go to the ladies' room to catch a bit of fresh air. All the girls were doing the same thing, leaning up against the stalls and moaning about Paul's beer breath or Craig's habit of spitting fountains of tobacco over Deb's shoulder.

Corey laughed and sat down on her bed. She stared at her black chicken boots. They were her father's. Everything she was wearing was her father's: her jeans tied around her waist with a nylon cord, her coat, her flannel shirt, her boots. She leaned over and pulled them off.

She walked over to her dresser, inched open the middle drawer and pulled out a white silk shawl. Her father had given it to her when she graduated from high school.

126

Melinda had made it for their wedding, but Corey hadn't worn it yet: not to Caruther's Bar, not to church, nowhere. She placed it on her pillow, walked back to her closet and pulled out the black dress she'd worn on her last date. She shook it, brushed off some lint, then threw it alongside the shawl and undressed. She tucked her father's clothes under her bed and out of sight. Then she slipped the dress over her head and zipped it up.

"Corey, is that you shuffling around?" her father called.

"That's me." She shut the closet door, and walked into his room.

He was sitting up, leaning against the mahogany headboard. He held *The Poultry Digest* in front of his face. "They say here they've come up with a new system for raising birds. Keeping them in cages." He coughed. "They say it cuts down on labor." He looked up over his magazine. "What's that?"

"I'm going into town with Lance tonight."

"What for?"

"No reason. Just because."

He looked back at his magazine and turned the page. "They say here that machines will be doing most of the work."

"I'll be home by nine."

"Won't need no outsiders."

"Father." Corey grabbed hold of the bedpost and shook it.

"Maybe you could work in a black dress." He closed the magazine, then shut his eyes and slipped underneath the quilt.

Corey turned and walked towards the door.

"Check on them birds before you go," he said as she touched the door knob.

Corey closed the door to the coops behind her. The chickens scurried away from her sound and headed towards the wall in a flock. She stood still and waited for them to calm down and adjust to her presence, then she knelt and touched the cedar chip mat. A lone chick pecked his way towards her searching for feed. Corey cupped her hand and reached out towards him, waiting, watching him cock his head left and then right. She knew he was thinking, thinking about her, watching her as if she was watching him. He stepped closer to her, jerking his head back and forth in synch with his movements. His beak poked her hand. It tickled and Corey laughed. The bird scurried back to the others.

Corey stood and walked alongside a feeder, staring down at her boots. The birds moved away from her, making a pathway, and inviting her into their flock. They had feathers now, white silk reaching up to her knees. The birds covered the floor, mulling up close to each other. Their beaks jabbed into the feeder, the chips. They were almost full grown. She noticed a dead bird, picked it up by its feet and let it hang down against her dress. She kept walking alongside the feeder, watching for dead or sick ones. When she reached the end of the house she turned and followed the opposite side of the feeder back to the far wall. She found six more dead birds, then headed to the side door and walked into the alcove. She stuffed them into a plastic bag, closed it tight so the smell wouldn't attract any coyotes, then placed it in a corner. She walked outside, glancing over at the incinerator. She should burn the dead ones, she thought, but there wasn't time.

Outside the coop, the air smelled of chickens, a combination of cedar chips that covered the floor and the chicks' own heat—a thick and gooey smell. Corey took a deep breath and slowly exhaled, then noticed Lance sitting in his pick-up in the dark. She walked over to him and knocked on his window. He nodded at her through the glass, then opened the door and got out. He was wearing a suit jacket and tie over jeans. Brown hair curled out from underneath a stetson hat and fell across his brow.

"Are you ready?" he asked.

She followed his eyes staring at her stomach moving along her legs to her feet. Feathers stuck to her. "You're early," she said.

"Not by much."

She wiped off her skirt, letting the white down float beside her. "You want to come inside?"

He shrugged and followed her into the house. She showed him the living room and watched him as he looked it over: the easy-boy where her father read before he went to bed stood next to the coal-burning stove; the standing ash tray he used as a spittoon; the brass container for wood; a leather two-seater sofa; the throw rugs on the wood floor. Lance walked over to the chair, sat down, and took out a cigarette.

"Where's your father?"

"Upstairs."

"You wearing those boots?"

She shook her head, turned around and headed upstairs. In her room, Corey put on a pair of black stockings and shoes, then she pulled out a bit of scotch tape from the drawer and with its sticky side collected up the feathers from her dress. She ran her hands through her hair, combing it, then wrapped the shawl around her shoulders and headed downstairs.

"Looking special, Corinda Gibb." He stood at the bottom of the stairs. When Corey reached the landing, he cupped her elbow under his hand and escorted her to his truck.

"Two of those specials," Lance said.

Corey sat on the barstool and turned it side to side in semi-circles. Her shoulder bumped against Lance's arm. The bartender slid a glass in front of her. She held it between her palms.

Lance nodded, picked up his own drink and gulped it down. "I'm not one for chickens like you are, Corinda."

"They're not bad." She tipped the glass back and forth, and watched the ice clink together.

"They're dumb."

"No more or less." She took a sip—gin and tonic. Her father drank gin and tonic, sipping it before he went to bed. He'd tighten the belt on his checkered bathrobe and tell her it was a nightcap. Once he was upstairs, Corey would hear the floorboards creak as he shuffled around his room. Then he'd start coughing, dragging his heart into his throat until there wasn't anything more to pull, until it was right there in his mouth. And he'd stop—stop until morning, when the hacking started again.

"Nothing's like that, Corinda. Nothing's ever no more or less."

"Is to me." She gave him a glance out of the corner of her eyes, watched him stare into his drink and stir the ice around with his finger. She pulled her shawl tight around her shoulders.

Lance looked at her. "Cold?"

"Just a shiver."

Lance looked away, staring at the bottles of liquor lining the wall behind the counter. "I won't be doing another loading. Going to leave."

"Where to?"

"Just out. I'm heading out."

"Oh." She pushed the glass away from her. It was making her cold, real cold. Shivers were spreading over her arms and down her spine. "That's a shame." She rubbed her arms. "You're a good worker."

He nodded again, picked up a piece of ice and popped it into his mouth. "It's just what I was thinking. Leaving here."

Corey swiveled her chair and touched her nylons against his jeans. He was hunched over his drink, protecting it. The skin on his face looked so smooth. She felt like brushing her hand along his chin, wondering if he had bristles like her father, bristles like the birds ready for loading. She dropped her hands onto her knees.

"Hey, Lance."

"Hey, Bob." Lance gripped the other man's hand.

"Don't see you down here often, Corey." Bob tapped her on the shoulder. "Looking good, though. Real good." He motioned the bartender with his hand. "Chickens okay?"

"Just fine."

"Must be if you're out." He nudged Lance. "Hey, boy. Is she sticking by you? I brought her here and I never could find her to dance."

"She's here." Lance pushed his glass away.

"Guess I didn't like it," Corey said and turned away from the two men. She fiddled with her drink.

"Bet you didn't too." He laughed. "Loading soon?"

"In three weeks."

"I hear your father's ill."

Corey nodded.

"I'll be around if you need help. Must be pretty lonely out in those coops." He hit Lance on his back, picked up his drink and headed across the bar.

She watched him sit down at a table with two other men, watched him slap them on the back and laugh. She took a sip of her drink, downing the last bit.

"I don't remember you going out with him," Lance said.

Corey turned towards him. "Once a while back. Why?"

"It don't figure with you, Corinda."

"Don't figure with what?"

"You're a finicky one." Lance rubbed his chin. "It took me a year to get you here."

"I don't like going out."

He took another gulp of his drink, then clinked it down on the counter when he was done. He turned towards her. Corey stared at her glass. "The other boys talk about you."

"Yeah?" She glanced up at him, caught his eye, then turned away again.

"They say you're in thick with your father. So thick he won't let you out." He put his hand on her shoulder. Corey turned her head. "But I say you're in thick with those birds."

"What difference does it make to you?" She kept her eyes locked onto his.

"No difference." He smiled and let his hand fall back onto the counter. "Just wondering."

"Wondering what?"

"Wondering why I never see you out with any men.

Wondering why I hear you danced with Bobby Hathaway at Caruthers. Wondering." He slid off his stool.

She watched him stuff his fingers into the pocket of his jeans, watched the lines around his mouth sink into a frown.

"So?"

"So I figured you're special, Corinda Gibb." He leaned against the bar. His hands slipped out of his pockets and fiddled with a napkin on the counter.

"What do you mean special?" she said.

"Just special, Corinda Gibb." He leaned towards her and placed a finger underneath her chin and tilted her head towards him. "Special like your name is special. Special like, Corinda Gibb."

Corey tipped over her drink. The ice slid out onto the counter and water dripped over the edge.

"Come on," he said and slipped his arm around her waist, then led her to the door.

He opened the car for her and she slid in, pulling her skirt over her knees. He slammed his door shut and turned the key in the ignition. He sat there, tapping the steering wheel with his fingers.

Corey played with the tassels on her shawl and looked at Lance's cheek. Lights from Caruther's Bar's parking lot flickered into the cab through the windshield.

Lance looked at her hands wrapping the yarn around her fingers then let his gaze drift up her arms to her face; he caught her eyes. He leaned forward and kissed her cheek, one side then the other. Their lips grazed each other, then pressed. She liked the feel of his soft warm skin against her cheek and she moved next to him. Lance fiddled with the buttons on her dress, slipped his hand under the material and over her breast. She slid her fingers into the back of his waistband, touched his skin, and then pulled him close.

"Hey, you two!" Bobby Hathaway pounded the hood. "What you doing in there?" He grinned at them.

Lance hit his fist on the dashboard. "Get out of here, Bobby," he said.

Corey pulled her shawl across her chest.

Bobby laughed, pounded the hood once more, and strode back towards the bar.

Corey stared after him. His shoulders swayed back and forth. She leaned against the car door. The armrest stuck into her side. "You going to take me home?" she said.

Lance leaned back into the seat and stared out the window.

A couple walked out of the bar and stood underneath the light. The boy lit up a cigarette, took a puff, then handed it to the girl. She held it between her fingers, leaned forward, and kissed him on the lips. She stepped back, laughing, then inhaled on the cigarette. She slipped the butt between her boyfriend's lips.

"You going to take me home?" Corey asked again.

Lance nodded, turned the key, switched gears, then backed the pick-up out of the parking lot.

The road to her home followed the farms. She saw both empty tilled fields, the gullies and hills left by the combines, waiting for a new season, and row after row of October corn—the flatness that extended on and on. Corey watched the telephone poles roll by her, one by one. She pretended to make the car stand still, watching the lines speed by. She liked doing things like that, liked reversing who was moving, pretending she was not. Her forehead rested against the window and felt cold against the glass.

Lance pulled into her driveway, stopped in front of her porch and turned off the motor.

"You want to come inside?" Corey asked.

"No. I should be getting home."

"It's early." She wiped the fringes of her shawl off her lap.

Lance held his keys in his hand, twirling them around and around. He turned towards her, stretched his arm across the back of the seat, and touched a strand of fringe on Corey's shawl. He twisted it around his fingers and leaned towards her.

Corey looked at him, then glanced away. Out of her window, she saw the lights from the chicken houses. She figured that he wanted another kiss and she thought about leaning over right then and there and kissing him full on the lips, but, instead, she reached for the door handle; she knew her father was waiting inside.

Lance followed her gaze. "Hey, there's a coyote," he said and pointed towards the far corner of the coop. A grey dog scooted around the chicken house and out of sight. "Hey!"

Corey jumped out of the pick-up and ran towards the chicken houses. She threw her shawl and heels into the mud.

"Hey, what are you doing?" Lance yelled.

Corey waved her arms up and down, shouting.

"Hey, be careful!" Lance ran after her.

Corey watched the coyote disappear behind the coops carrying a bird in his mouth; white feathers trailed behind it. She flapped her arms once more then stopped, walked over to the wall of the house and leaned against it.

Lance caught up to her.

"They smelled the dead ones. I didn't burn the dead ones." She pushed Lance out of her way and walked around the coop to the side door. It was ajar. Inside the plastic bag was open. The remains of the dead chickens were spread on the floor. She walked over to the door leading to the chickens and opened it. The birds were huddled over to the far side of the house. She stepped into the cedar chips, swinging her arms back and forth, and cooed. She motioned Lance to mimic her on the other side of the coop.

She saw Lance step into the house, lift his arms up flapping, and watched the birds scurry away from his movement, leaving trampled birds behind. He kept walking around the house until he met Corey on the opposite side. Then he followed her alongside the feeders. He picked up the birds and carried them to the alcove, making a heap on the floor, back and forth, again and again. He stuck his arm out straight and stiff, and held the carcasses away from his body. Corey motioned him into the alcove. He followed her and shut the door.

She gathered up the birds and headed over to the incinerator. She flipped on the gas, listened for a pop, then opened the door and threw in a few birds. She moved out of the way and let Lance toss in his bundle. A smell of rotten egg and burnt flesh rose up in smoke. Corey threw in the last bird, shut the hatch, then walked to the porch and sat on the steps.

"Corey?" Her father coughed out. He stood up against the screen and peered out.

Corey stood up, pulled the door open, and let her father lean on her shoulder as he stepped towards her. "You shouldn't be up," she said.

"Coyotes?" he whispered.

"Coyotes."

"How many did we lose?"

"Around two hundred."

He wheezed and leaned hard on her shoulder. "How'd they get inside?" he said.

"I must have left the door unlatched."

He shook his head.

"Left the dead ones out too," she added and walked onto the porch, ushering her father along with her. She heard the screen door slam behind her.

"Evening, Mr. Gibb." Lance put one foot on the steps moving out from the shadows into the porch light. Feathers stuck to his jeans and he brushed them off.

Her father nodded at Lance, wheezed, then tightened his grip on Corey's shoulder. He pinched her skin. He walked forward, his step faltering.

Lance grabbed his arm and held him stable.

Her father coughed again, a deep cough, cupping his hand over his mouth. When he pulled it away, Corey saw a thick chunk of blood smeared on his palm. She glanced over her father's white tufts and caught Lance's look. They turned him around and walked him up the steps. Corey held her father under his elbow and watched his feet; they slid onto each step scuffing across the wood like a skate on rough ice; then his foot caught the ledge and he fell forward. Lance and Corey caught him before he touched the steps, his hands in front of him preparing to catch his fall.

"You okay, Mr. Gibb?" Lance asked.

"Mmm," he said, his voice gruff. He leaned down and touched the ledge, his hand rubbing the wood like sandpaper.

In his bedroom, Corey tucked the bed sheets around her father, then brushed her hand over his cheek, following the cracks from his mouth.

"You sleep now," she said.

He coughed, a dry one this time, filling out his cheeks with air. Corey lifted him up and pushed the pillows behind his back. Lance slipped out the door.

"Isn't right," her father said.

"Never is."

"Isn't right you're doing this all alone." He stuck his neck out, making the veins bulge out. "Isn't right you're taking care of them without me."

"It happens."

"Shouldn't. Shouldn't be working all alone." He closed his eyes and leaned back into the pillows.

"I could do worse," she said.

He moved down underneath the covers. "You could," he said.

Corey touched his closed eyes and followed the cracks that trailed off them, tracing her fingertips along the lines until they disappeared. They seemed like the skin of dead birds, loose and spongey, slipping from her grip as she held them by their legs. She combed her fingers through her father's hair, then leaned down and kissed his forehead.

"You check on them birds before you head to sleep," he said. His eyes were still shut and his lips hardly moved. "And look for coyotes." His voice faded and Corey turned the light off as she closed his door.

Downstairs, Lance sat in the easy-boy, fiddling with her shawl. "I brought these in for you." He held out her shoes and shawl. They were covered with mud.

"Thank you." Corey took them from Lance and put them on the sofa. She sat down across from him.

Lance leaned forward and rested his elbows on his knees. "He's okay?" He looked straight into her eyes, then dropped his gaze down to her feet; her stockings, splattered with mud, were dotted with cedar chips.

"Asleep," she said and put her hands on her knees.

"I'm awfully sorry about your father," he said and stood up, tugging down on his jeans. When she didn't stand up too, he added, "I should be going. I'm getting up early." He cleared his throat.

Corey slipped her hands underneath her thighs.

"I got a ride to Chicago. I didn't tell you that earlier," he said. "But I'm going to Chicago."

"What's in Chicago?" she asked and squeezed her arms against her ribs.

"I don't know," he said. "I've got a cousin in Chicago."

"Oh." Her dress was covered with chicken feathers and she started to pick them off, dropping the white fluff onto the floor. When Corey looked up again, Lance was fiddling with her father's tumbler of gin, holding the glass up to his eye as if he were trying to see what was inside, but it was empty. "I got to check around the coops for coyotes," she said. "I'll walk you outside." She stood up.

Lance nodded and put the glass back on the edge of the spittoon.

Corey brushed against him as she walked passed Lance to the door. The floor boards creaked under the rattan rug. In the foyer, she put on a pair of her father's boots, sitting on newspaper, on the floor. Lance held the screen door open for her. They walked to his truck. The night sky was clear and Corey searched for the Big Dipper.

"Maybe you'd like to come?" he asked as he reached his truck. His hand fiddled with the keys in his pocket.

"To Chicago?" She shook her head. "I couldn't go to Chicago," she added, then shivered. She had forgotten to wear her shawl.

He put his hand on her elbow and pulled her into his arms.

He rubbed her back, trying to warm her. "Why not?" he asked.

"I don't know." She looked at him and their eyes met for a moment before Corey stared at the ground, at his cowboy boots with feathers and mud on the side of the heel. She tried to imagine Lance going away and not returning, but she couldn't. Instead, she saw him loading the chickens onto trucks bound for market. He'd hand her four chickens, all held by their legs, and she'd put them into a cage, again and again until the truck was piled high with cages full of squacking birds and all the coops were empty and ready for the new load of day-olds. She saw this picture as clear as she saw Lance in front of her. "Maybe you'd like to stay?" she asked.

"I don't know," he said, then added, "No, I couldn't." He folded his arms across his chest.

Corey stepped back and folded her arms across her chest like Lance. "I left my shawl inside," she said. Lance didn't move. "I got to check for coyotes," she added, then she touched his arm. "You stop by before you leave," she said.

He shook his head. "I can't," he said. "I'm leaving early." He opened the car door and started to sit down inside the pick-up, but stopped and turned back to Corey. He pulled her towards him and kissed her on the lips, then he stepped back and nodded at her, touching his fingers to the tip of his hat. "You take care of yourself," he said and shut the door.

Corey waited by the pick-up while Lance started the engine and flicked on the headlights. She rubbed her arms, over goosebumps, and watched him head down the drive-way to the road before she headed around the coops. The ground was hard and Corey kicked chunks of dirt; one piece sprung loose and hit the aluminum wall of the coop. The chickens balked inside and Corey ran to the side door worried that she'd frightened them.

The birds were feeding, mulling about and poking at the cedar chip matting. She clapped her hands, trying to push a clump of chickens away from the wall, but the birds refused to move; she pushed them with her boot. Along the far wall, one bird lay dead under a water bell, its feathers wet and matted against a small frame. Corey picked the chicken up by its legs and continued walking around the coop until she had made a full circle. The bird bounced against her leg, its beak poking her knee. In the alcove, she stuffed it into a plastic bag and tied it shut with a piece of string, then covered the bag with a piece of tarp. Once outside the coop, she secured the latch on the door. She walked towards her house, dark except for her bedroom light. The night was still and Corey only heard her boots crunching against the frozen dirt—a hollow thud-thud, thud-thud—that made Corey quicken her pace until she was inside her house, the door closed behind her and up the stairs, safely standing by her father's bed.

REBECCA ANN JORNS

Coming of Age

I DON'T REMEMBER when Daddy went away to Viet Nam the first time. There was no long drive to the airport, no sad goodbyes or lots of hugging. I don't remember Mom telling us. A few days went by and I just thought he hadn't come home from work yet. It wasn't until Pam and I got in a fight and I yelled, "Oh yeah? Well just wait till Dad comes home!" that I learned Daddy wasn't coming home for a very long time. Mom settled the argument by making us stare at each other until we could speak nicely to the other person. "Honestly, I just don't understand you girls. Pam's the only sister you'll ever have, Shelley. And Shelley's the only sister you'll ever have, Pamela. You two have a very special relationship."

I thought everybody's daddy was in Viet Nam until the weekend Mom took us shopping at Lenox Square and I saw lots of dads. Some pushed strollers, others held hands with little children my age, some were with kids older than Pam. But there they all were: everyone's dads with everyone's moms. I searched the faces in the crowd to see if maybe my dad was in there somewhere, but he wasn't. My dad was missing.

It's not a typical life growing up in the Army. Georgia was the first time we lived off-post, and it was in Georgia that I gradually learned that not every kid's dad was in Viet Nam, or even wanted to be. In fact, a lot of dads weren't even in the army. How strange, I thought. Didn't every daddy wear fatigues and army boots and leave home every so often for months or even a year? One of Pam's teachers sent home a note that read: "I've just heard about your husband. This must be such a difficult time for you." But life went on, even when Daddy was halfway across the globe helping people do things I still don't really understand. Still, life back home continued. It had to; and Mom made sure it did.

There was a large white dogwood in front of our yard, the grassy hill sloping down to meet the road and our gray mailbox with the bent flag. Months later we three danced around the mailbox, eyeing the red-white-and-blue Jeep up the road and Sam, the mailman, who every month or so brought a package. Sometimes we'd dance about, see Sam drive up, and he'd just say, "Sorry kids, junk mail today. Maybe tomorrow," and drive away. But usually Sam did not let us down. Usually he had a box wrapped in masking tape with "To the Krueger Family" written across in black.

"Hey, that's us!" exclaimed Pam, taking the package. "It's for us!" And we raced after her up the hill to show Mom who, if it was fall, was usually inside writing.

"Open it, open it!" we shouted. "It's from Dad! Hurry!" Mom set aside her writing, a ragged pile of scribbles, pushed away a strand of hair, and opened the box. "Is there gum?" I asked, standing beside her.

"There's always gum," Pam stated, matter-of-factly.

"Is not," Larry said.

Daddy usually put three sticks of Wrigley's in the packages and we spent the better part of the afternoon peeling the shiny foil from the gooey gum. I don't know why we did. Mom had gum in the kitchen drawer where the rubber-bands from the Sunday paper were. I guess this gum was different. This was gum from Viet Nam. It was special gum, even though it lost its flavor fast and felt like slime. Once I swallowed mine by accident. It just slid right down like water.

"Oh yuck, Shelley! That's gonna take your guts fifty years to eat that!" said Pam, pretending to be nauseated.

I didn't know Daddy much and I didn't get to know him any better from his letters. Each child got a paragraph addressed especially to him, but each one sounded the same. "Good luck in school," "Golly, you're getting so tall," "Help your mother while I'm away." These were the letters Mom could read to us. These were the real ones. Sometimes we'd run a letter up, sit on the stoop, pick our gum, but Mom wouldn't call us in to read. When I asked her why once, her eyes got glassy and she said, "Because it's not a real letter this time."

In the corners of the letters was always a number with a circle around it so that Mom knew the order Daddy sent the letters. Sort of. She got #37 before #34 and later received #29 which was in response to her #21. Still, Mom put a lot of faith in those numbers. They meant something to her.

"Oh," I said, not understanding.

"Shelley," Pam said, squatting to look me in the face, "there are real letters and not-real letters and this one is not real." She turned to Mom. "Right?"

"Right dear," Mom said, her eyes puffy.

Pam was eleven after all so I figured she probably knew about this real and not-real stuff. When I told Larry he said, "What? That isn't right. That doesn't make sense." But when he asked Mom she told him just what Pam told me.

Much later I was to learn what Mom meant by those letters. Not-real letters were addressed to "Francine," my mother's full birth name which she never used. Should Daddy be in trouble, he addressed all letters to Francine. The mail was no doubt torn open and read before it left the country, so Daddy was sure to avoid specifics. In his letters to Francine, though, Daddy's imagination was at its best: "birds fly toward the ground like thick black ashes" (meaning that there had been heavy aerial bombing); "the river runs cool and wide" (Viet Cong maneuvers were widespread in the area); "clouds drift over us like ghosts in the wind" (radio communication had been lost).

Letters to Frannie or Fran were usually bitter discourses on the "bastard Generals" or "damn enlistees shooting up" or the "shit weather," except of course the three paragraphs devoted to us, my father's children; words that Daddy believed were words to live by. Help your mother. Do well in school. Words that never came alive for us because the man who wrote them did not seem alive to us. He was like Santa Claus: we thought about him every once in a while, but then we sort of forgot. Even Santa got crowded out in a child's mind by other things, more important things, things worth thinking about.

The day Dad came home was like any other, except that I was counting the days to my sixth birthday: only four more. Mom acted strange that day. For the first time in a long time we had to clean the house—every inch of it, even under our beds. Mrs. Casper came over to watch us when Mom left to "pick up someone special" which I thought meant Bugs Bunny (whom I had seen in person at Sears the day before). I tingled at the thought of getting Bugs for my birthday and wished that school wasn't out so I could tell my class. Mrs. Casper had us watch TV so we wouldn't get dirty and mess up the house. It was too early for cartoons so she turned the channel to the soap opera she watched. It was boring. People fought and kissed a lot and there were no kids. When I asked Mrs. Casper if I could play outside instead she said no, I'd get my hair messed up. Well of course, I'd get my hair messed up. That was part of the fun, wasn't it? I grew impatient with the endless kissing and detergent commercials and why I couldn't go outside on a perfectly wonderful day. Mom loved it when we played outside; in fact, she preferred it. So what was old Mrs. Casper's trouble?

Hearing the front door open, I walked through the dining room, asking, "Hey Mom, can I go out—?" but when I reached the living room there stood in the doorway not just

Mom, but a big man in green wearing a hat.

"Children!" Mom called, smiling happily. "Someone is here to see you!"

Larry came in first, walked slowly over to the man and looked up into the unfamiliar face. "You're Viet Nam."

The man chuckled, knelt down to the ground, said, "Lar, I'm not a country. I'm your father."

"You're Dad?" I asked, looking at Mom who now had stopped smiling. He didn't look like Dad, but then again, it had been so long since I had seen Dad. He was a fragment in a few memories. In one, I saw a face; in another, a part of a face; in another, just a shadow, like Dad had faded, which he had, but now Dad was back, in living color in my living room. So this was Dad.

Pam ran out, saw Dad and squealed, "Oooh Daddy, it's you!" and hugged him around his bristled neck. Of course, she would remember Dad, she was older. She remembered.

That night Dad set up the slide projector in the TV room and flashed pictures of Viet Nam against the wall. He showed us holes in the dirt that looked just like the ones in our backyard, a road he said was an airstrip, and bridges that looked like they were made with Lincoln Logs. The pictures were gray and some were out of focus. Larry liked the slides and said he wanted to be an engineer someday, too. Mom was uneasy during the show and smoked cigarettes. In one picture, Dad was next to a dead dog by a ditch.

"This here is Max. Max got killed and I buried him in that hole."

"Oooh, you didn't pick him up with your hands, did you?" Larry asked, screwing up his face.

"Of course I picked him up," Dad said, clicking to the next slide. "Had to bury him, didn't I?"

"Mom told us not to touch dead things," I said.

Mom and Dad exchanged looks. She stared at him steadily with eyes pinched from cigarette smoke drifting by. "She told you kids that, huh," Dad finally said, their eyes still locked. Mom inhaled deeply and the end of her cigarette glowed like fiery ambers. "Well, that's a good lesson to learn," he said. Mom exhaled, and smoky spirals unravelled across the black and white pictures on the wall. "But you see where I was," Dad explained, "it was okay to touch dead things."

For a long moment, the hum of the projector filled the black room and we were quiet.

Things changed after Dad came home. Suddenly we had a bedtime, even on Fridays and Saturdays, and we had to go to church on Sundays. Every Sunday. Dad liked to sing at church, said he used to be in the Portage United Methodist Choir when he was a boy, but now Dad just sang loudly from the pew, his index finger skimming the bars of music in the worn hymnal, his voice bellowing forth, making the wooden bench tremble, and drowning out the other voices. During service, Larry and I drew pictures on the bulletin and giggled at the old ladies' hats with the plastic fruit and birds. Way up front was the altar and the man in a black robe who read from a mustard-colored book that sat on a mustard-colored stand. In fact, the entire church was mustard-colored: the carpet, curtains, choir robes, hymnals. After service, Dad always shook the minister's hand and said he enjoyed the sermon. I shook the minister's hand once. It felt like Mom's after she rubbed Jergens on them, except his didn't smell.

After Dad was home, a few more letters from Viet Nam trickled in with the junk mail. I had a hard time understanding how letters could still be coming when Dad was home. I thought maybe Dad went back to Viet Nam at night to write to us and send us gum. And in the morning, he returned to be with us in our house. For a while, I thought Dad was God because they were both fathers. Our father, thou art in heaven. Every month or so another letter came. Mom didn't read them to us. She just skimmed them, and threw them out. Maybe the letters were from heaven and this wasn't really Dad here but God. Maybe Dad was in heaven, writing to us. But at age six, I didn't know what to think. For all I knew, Viet Nam was a heaven, and mailmen were angels, and letters were reminders that there was a father, somewhere, even in heaven.

"Who put these glasses away!" Dad's voice shook the house like thunder.

"Frank, what's the matter?" Mom called, going into the kitchen, tying her bathrobe tighter. We three held our breath in the TV room.

"For Chrissakes, since when do little glasses go behind the *big* glasses?" Dad shouted. "The kids didn't *used* to put 'em away like this!"

"They probably forgot," Mom replied, matter-of-factly.

"Only one way a kid forgets," Dad muttered, stomping into the TV room, and glaring at us with wild eyes, pointing at Larry with a blood-tipped finger. "You! You, young man, had kitchen duty, correct?"

"Yessir."

"Do you know what happens when you don't put little cups in *front* of big ones?"

"Uh, no sir." Larry's voice quivered.

Dad waved his finger around. "People drop things. Things break. People get hurt. Understand?"

"Frank, stop it!" Mom shouted, hands on hips. "It's your own fault that glass dropped."

"I'm just teaching them a lesson, Fran. It's common sense to do it this way."

Mom's eyes flashed like lightning. "We got along fine without your common sense." The room felt suddenly cramped as we three sat petrified on the stiff sofa, eyes glued on our mother and dad, hearts pumping inside us, almost bursting out.

"I can't help it if I'm not around all the time," Dad snapped. "But Jesus, I didn't expect to come back to *this*."

Tension crackled in the room. Mom, without looking at us, told us children to leave. We sprang from the sofa and scrambled over one another to the living room.

"Boy, they're really going at it," Pam whispered, her voice shaky. We listened to the noise that made the floor and the wall tremble.

"No, I think you rather enjoy dumping us off in the middle of nowhere while you stomp out other people's problems."

"You don't know anything, you know that? You don't even know what I did over there!"

"I know you did more than lay airstrips."

Silence. For a long time, nothing.

"What are they doing?" I asked, frightened.

"Shhh!" Pam said, leaning closer to hear. The back door slammed and shook the mirror above the mantle. Mom came in through the dining room, saw the backs of us.

"Been listening in, have you?" she said, making us jump up.

"Hard not to, Mom," Larry confessed, looking at the ground.

"Who won?" I asked, half expecting the house to begin vibrating again.

Mom scooped us up in her arms. "No one wins," she said.

"But you had a fight, didn't you?" Larry asked.

"Oh yes," she sighed. "We had a fight. But no one ever wins."

As she tucked me into bed, Mom kissed my cheek and said softly, "You kids are my life." Then she walked to the doorway and turned off the overhead light. In the black of the room, I tossed in bed. "Shelley," Pam said, in an unusually nice voice, "try to go to sleep."

That night I dreamt Mom was in a big green field of tall wispy grass and the kids were waiting by a tree for a mailman—who never came. When we ran to tell Mom, she began pulling up the grass and throwing it high in the sweet air, laughing, "Have you ever seen green rain?" She kept throwing the grass up toward the wide blue sky and we three danced around her, singing, "Ha ha ha, have you ever seen green rain?" The sky was full of green grass but before long, instead of grass coming down, pieces of spearmint Wrigley's were, hundreds of 'em, and all you had to do was slip off the wrapper and slide it in your mouth. That's all we did out there in the field was laugh and dance and chew our gum, and the gum never lost its flavor, it just kept tasting better.

I think of that time now as I walk in the oppressive mugginess of Washington, D.C. I quit school when Dad got stationed here so I could march downtown for ERA. My dreams have changed since I was a six-year-old girl. Caton Hills hadn't even heard of ERA and my college friends thought feminism was a word mentioned only in hushed voices in the privacy of the dorm elevator. For me, Washington means opportunity.

Mom doesn't embrace ERA either, but she thinks I'm brave to believe in something. At breakfast, she burns the toast and when I reach for the Cheerios there are only a few loops trapped in the crinkles of wax paper lining. We decide just to drink coffee and talk. Mom giggles about old boyfriends and what she wanted to be when she grew up. When do you know you're grown up? Mom thinks she's passed by "grown up" and I guess for that reason her dreams will just be dreams. Mom says if she had married Buddy Schuester, she'd be a veterinarian's wife in Portage, Wisconsin. But she also adds that she wouldn't want to be on a farm with a husband who smelled of cow manure and horse hair. I tell her about the cute guy who marches downtown with me. He makes the marches tolerable, and fun. I hadn't counted on D.C. summers being so humid. If it weren't for Zach, I would be tempted to hop back in the air-conditioned taxi, go home, and find some other way to annoy Dad. "Yes," Mom says, chuckling, "you do like to annoy your father." She and Bud Schuester were voted Cutest Couple in twelfth grade, but he was vet-school bound after graduation and Mom didn't want to wait. Besides, Portage was a small town and getting smaller. One of her girlfriends enlisted in the Air Force and was stationed in Greenland. Mom says she dreamt for weeks about Greenland and how wonderfully different it must be. That summer, she married Dad. Mom puts her face in the napkin and cries.

"C'mon, Mom. It's all right."

"What have I done? What have I got to show for myself?"

"Mother, you have three terrific kids. I know a lot of

women who would gladly switch places with you." That's a lie. In the crowd I run around with, I don't know of one woman who would envy my mother.

"But you kids don't need me anymore. Larry's finally going to school after all these years; and you, you've found your niche now; and Pam has her own family now. What is there for me? What's left for Fran?"

I reach for her hand. "If you want a job, Mom, you go out and get one. You'd make one helluva business woman."

When I was six, Mom made me a ballerina costume for Halloween. I was in pink tights with a tutu of netting and a diamond tiara that Pam made sure to tell me was really only rhinestones. Pam was Bat Girl and Larry was G.I. Joe. On Halloween night, we three sat anxiously at the dinner table, wishing darkness upon our neighborhood so we could begin our trick-or-treating. A knock made us jump, and when Mom opened the door to a small throng of giggling children, she could hardly make us wait till seven o'clock. "Okay," she relented. "But you turn around at the MacGruders' and come straight home, understand? No crossing the intersection." Yeah, yeah, we said, and skipped down the sidewalk. As the only male, Larry appointed himself leader. As the oldest child, Pam appointed herself leader. As the baby of the family, I followed. I was always the follower. Larry and Pam lead me all over that neighborhood and Larry was all set to cross the street after visiting Mr. MacGruder's but Pam said she'd tattle and knowing Pam, she would.

I had a commissary bag full of candy. Mom threw out the items she said might be poisoned or tampered. Out went the apples, which didn't upset me much, but when she emptied my bag of every homemade chocolate I almost cried. Still, there was plenty of candy left to swap with Larry and Pam. I hated anything with peanut butter so Larry got my Reese's cups and those peanut butter chews I think only Larry liked. Pam got my Jolly Ranchers in exchange for her Zots and Rock Candy. We each coveted our Tootsie Pops. Some things cannot be bargained. At dinner the next night, Mom told stories about when we three were little. Like in Heidelberg when Larry was in kindergarten at All Saint's Grammar School and one of the nuns told Mom that Larry had to call her "Sister" Marie and not "Mrs." Marie. Even though Mom explained that we were not Catholic and Larry was at the school only to learn German, Sister Marie insisted that he adjust. Weeks went by and Larry was still calling Sister Marie "Mrs." Finally, during a conference, Sister asked Larry just when he intended on calling her by her correct name and Larry said, "When you stop calling me Harry," so that was the end of that. Mom likes telling stories around the dinner table. They made her happy and we laughed a lot. Most of them I didn't understand, but I knew when to laugh. It's not hard to know when to laugh.

I realize now that Mom didn't want encouragement at breakfast to find a job. She wanted me to tell her that she didn't need a job, that she was a good mother who should be happy to work at home. Here I push for women in the business world when the hardest working woman I know is tying back overbearing tomato plants in her garden.

That Sunday, Mom tells Larry that he needs to clear out junk from the shed that he doesn't want anymore. After all, the man is twenty-three, he can't want *all* of that stuff. Dad has his nose in the *Washington Post* when Larry comes through with a box of old toys. Dad peeks over the top of the front page.

"What are you doing with those?" he asks.

"Giving 'em to Salvation Army."

"Salvation Army? Hell, that's *real* army stuff. There's the tank I gave you and the renovated helicopter and here's the five-ton tractor—"

"Dad, they were just toys."

The man with peppered sideburns looks offended. "They may be 'just toys' to you, but they're important equipment to me. Why, if it weren't for this here bulldozer there wouldn't have been a trail to Cambodia."

"Fine. You play with 'em." And Larry drops the box at his feet. The rattle distresses my father; he looks at me.

I go upstairs to Larry's room. Mom brought home some

large brown boxes with "New Freedom" printed on the side.

"Gee, Lar," I say. "You'll put Playtex outta business the rate you buy this stuff."

"Very funny. Hey, what should I do with all these pictures? I bet if you put 'em together and flipped 'em it could be a video of our family, kinda."

"Shit, that would stink."

"You cuss too much."

"You don't cuss enough," I say.

"You want these or should I give 'em to Mom?"

"She'd just throw darts at the ones of Dad."

"I don't have many of Dad," he says.

When I cut through the den to go outside, I pause to watch my father glue a wing back on a busted bomber.

"This is a B-29," he says, holding it up.

"Just looks like a plane to me."

He calls after me outside. "It *is* a plane, you!" But I pretend not to hear. I couldn't even joke with Dad—Jesus, did he think I was serious? Somewhere along the way, Pop lost his sense of humor and I wonder if maybe he didn't accidentally bury it beneath a road going to Cambodia.

Larry comes out with another load. We walk side by side down the long, asphalt drive to the curb and that's when he says I should go back to school, too.

I snort with laughter. "Now why would I want to do that?"

"To do something. To be somebody."

In a dramatic move, I place my hands on my breast and say, "But I am doing something—I'm finding myself."

"Cut it out. I'm serious. I know you, Shelley, and you don't have a purpose in life. You're smart but nobody'd know it. You should get out and do something important. And I don't mean those dumb marches. You don't believe in all that." We walk up the drive and I spot Mom crouched over her garden.

"Hey Mom!" I call to her. "Lar says I gotta get out and do stuff. Whaddya suppose I oughta do?"

She rolls her eyes, waves me off with the back of her orange-gloved hand. Larry's wrong. He doesn't know me. My ERA marches are all I need. Getting up every morning gives my day a purpose; and ticking off Dad gives me that much-needed sense of accomplishment.

That night, Mom and I sit alone at the dinner table. Larry is out. Dad's not home yet.

"Where's Dad?"

"I think he had a briefing tonight," Mom says.

"On Sunday?"

"He's probably preparing for the briefing."

"Mom, it's after nine."

"Honey, he works late. You know that. He likes to be by himself at the office to work."

"You have no idea where Dad is, do you."

She lights a cigarette. Her eyes turn cloudy.

"God damn him," I mutter, throwing the fork down.

Mom begins to cry. "Please don't say those things."

"Mother, how can you just sit there? Doesn't it bother you? Don't you want to do something?"

She doesn't answer, just holds her lit cigarette and wipes her eyes.

Upstairs in my bedroom, I wait in the dark for Dad to come home. I listen for the car, for the creak of the front door. Hours go by. I hear nothing.

Monday morning, I go to Dad's office at the Pentagon. I was supposed to march again today, but I haven't been in over a week. It's just not the same. Nothing is the same. An overweight security guard asks me for an I.D. and I dig to the bottom of my duffle bag in search of the dependent I.D. I haven't used since high school. I find it sandwiched between an expired library card from Kentucky and an awful picture of a high school boyfriend. I flash the beige card in front of the guard, but when I step inside I see that it expired on my eighteenth birthday, two years ago.

I look in a directory for Dad's room number and then a map to figure how to find Dad's room number. I walk down ramps, up steps, round and round in pentagonal circles.

Finally, I reach the fourth floor and the eighth corridor. The floor is covered in shiny black and white linoleum and the wall is lined with gaudily framed portraits of important people. Dad's hall looks better than the others I've seen. I walk right in the office, see his back at a desk in front of me.

"Hey Colonel." He turns around, stricken. The other men say hi, smile. My father is flushed. "Gotta minute, Dad?" He hurries me out the door, and when we are a safe distance away from the office, he gasps, "What are you doing here?"

"Embarrassed?"

"Of course I'm embarrassed. What are you doing here?"

"Dad. Why is it the only way I can get your attention is when I catch you off guard?"

"Get to the point."

"Okay. You're a bastard."

He lets out a long sigh, letting me know that I've taken him away from something important. "Michelle, if you mean that I haven't been a father to you and the kids, I understand. I've had to make certain sacrifices to get where I am, but I still think I provide for my family."

"You haven't got a family."

He glances back at his watch. "If this is all you wanted to discuss with me, I've got work to do."

"Oh, I figured you would've finished all your work last night." He stares at me, stunned. "Did I catch you off guard again?" He turns to walk down the checkboard-floored corridor and I call after the man in green. "You know, Dad, you may think you're a hot-shot hero. But Mom's the real survivor."

That night, Dad brings home red roses wrapped in green wax paper for Mother. On the plain white card, he wrote: For You. Mom puts them in a crystal vase, sets them on the table, but they aren't nearly as beautiful as the golden chrysanthemums and fiery zinnias in her backyard. And finally, I think Mom knows it. She and I sit at the table, alone, looking at the roses.

"I honestly didn't expect him back tonight," she confesses. Her eyes are fixed on the flowers. "I certainly didn't expect those."

"What did you expect, Mom?"

She takes a long drag on a cigarette, lets it out slowly, casually. "I expected the world. I deserved that once." She takes a rose from the vase, plucks off a petal one at a time. Did she ever do that as a child? He loves me. He loves me not.

"What now? What are you going to do?"

"The roses? I'll keep adding sugar to the water, but they'll be dead by the end of the week. This vase is too large for them anyway." She finishes plucking the petals from the rose. Deep red petals cover the table. Petals that curl at the edges. My mother looks at them, then says to herself, "make a wish," and with a tilt of her head blows the rose petals away. As they drift across the table and fall gently to the floor, my mother smiles, her eyes closed. She keeps them closed for a long time, and I think, this is how I want to remember my mother. Making a wish and closing her eyes just long enough to make that wish happen. She deserves that. My mother deserves a million moments like this.

MARGARET PETERSON HADDIX

Ash

THE FIRE STARTS as soon as I shut my eyes. In seconds it is licking my mattress and sheets, reaching for my arms and legs. The smoke is in my mouth and burning down to my lungs. My feet are on fire, my hands, my face.

I open my eyes. The hospital room is full of shadow, not flames. *It didn't happen.* I try to bring my hand to touch my face, to prove it. But I am covered in gauze. My elbows won't bend. *It did happen. It just didn't happen that way.*

I peer at twenty-four rectangles hung on the concrete block wall, get-well cards made by my third-graders. Above them, moonlight and light from the street shove past the window blinds and land on my sheets. I can almost move my feet beneath them.

The smoke scent is still in my nose, but I do not call for the nurse this time.

The first time the night nurse humored me, lifted the sheets, looked under my bed: "See? No fire here. You dreamed about your fire. That's over." The second time she was firmer. "We have alarms to catch those things. We have a

monitor on all the rooms—I watch you all night. You're safe."
She gave me a stronger sleeping pill.

I found out after that: my nose smells only smoke now.
Julie brought me chocolate chip cookies, hot and straight
from the oven. I could not smell them. The nurses complain
that my salve stinks, but I cannot tell. My nose can only
remember what it smelled the last time it was normal.

In the morning they put me in a tank of water and pull off
my dead skin. Debriding, it's called. It hurts worse than the
fire did.

"Did you have your dream last night?" the nurse asks.

"Yes."

I know all the nurses now. This one's name is Angie; she
has curly blonde hair and a turned-up nose and she acts like
skinless flesh is normal. But she's as gentle as possible, considering, and she knows what not to talk about.

"Your hand is looking good here," she says as she scrubs at
my fingertip. "It'll probably be ready for a graft soon."

My hand is red, grotesque. But I can pretend I approve of
it.

"Just so it's not pigskin you give me. Or on second
thought—I could probably keep the kids in awe of me with a
pigskin hand. Discipline would be easy that way."

Angie laughs. I have scored points for being a good
sport.

"No, this would be your skin. From there." She points to
my thigh, my one expanse of unburned skin. So it is to be
scarred, too.

"You guys make sure everything is ruined, don't you?"

For a moment I think I may have lost my good sport status.
But she nods grimly.

"Don't think we enjoy it."

On the radio above the debriding tank, Bruce Springsteen
rasps about his hometown dying. I feel my throat catch, and
before I can stop it, a tear rolls onto my burned cheek.

"This song always gets me," I say.

Angie nods. Maybe she believes me; maybe not.

"How big is—where do you teach?"

"Lyle. It's tiny. But that's not my hometown. Just where I could get a job."

"Where are you from?"

"Pittsburgh."

The word makes me picture my parents' living room: stiff green couches, faded-flower wallpaper, a rug the color of nothingness. Mom had framed some cardboard paintings her grocery store gave away, mainly dreary, badly done imitations of pre-Impressionist art. I had hated that room. Now I longed for it.

My parents were going to come out after the fire, but I told them no. I knew they couldn't afford to. I knew that if I saw them, one of them would say by mistake, "If you'd come back to Pittsburgh, this wouldn't have happened."

It was true.

I had struggled so long to decide. Even when the choice became a job in Lyle, Indiana, or a job in Pittsburgh, my former college roommate Julie was persuasive.

"You'll only be an hour from me—you can see a lot of me and Steve and Bob and everyone. It'll be like college never ended."

I was staying with her after my interview in Lyle. She was already working in Chicago, doing public relations for Marshall Fields and exulting about her job, her co-workers, her salary.

"What's your life going to be like in Pittsburgh?" she said.

"Dull," I muttered. "But—Lyle, Indiana? What could possibly happen there?"

"It will be a change. You have to look for excitement in life, right? Maybe you'll find a job up here after a year. And then, who knows?" Julie flipped a strand of long, red hair over her shoulder. She grinned at me, confidently.

I looked around her airy apartment. She already had a matching creme couch and chair, red and blue dried strawflowers in vases around the room, huge prints of ballerinas on the walls. It seemed a symbol to be compared with a nothing-colored rug and depressing forged paintings. I am not superficial, but—I was then.

And I was to be burned in Julie's apartment.

Angie finishes peeling off my layers of skin, smoothes on the salve I cannot smell and wraps me in gauze again. I am a mummy lying on my bed, waiting to be peeled and wrapped again.

It is an endless cycle. I have been here a week, two weeks—three? I cannot remember. I cannot remember what it was like to be a normal person, without fiery nightmares, with smooth skin and hands and feet that do not throb.

"Ready for lunch?"

Mike, the nurse's aide, brings in a tray and sits down to feed me.

"How are we doing today?"

"Fine," I lie.

He props me up and slides the table around so the tray is below my chin.

The tray holds more than I can eat: hamburgers, French fries, green beans, mixed fruit, a milkshake. It reminds me of school food—the stuff I always had to coax little Heather Wilson to eat. Now Mike coaxes me.

"You need all these calories to heal," he tells me. "It takes a lot of energy to regenerate skin."

He shovels the beans into my mouth. I cannot taste them, but they stick in my throat. I cough, almost gag. A bean falls into the folds of bandages across my chin.

"I'm sorry," I whisper, as ashamed as poor Heather, kept in from recess because she will not eat.

Mike lets the fork clatter on the plate, picks the bean out of the gauze.

"I can't eat anymore," I tell him.

"Maybe a treat? Angie stopped at Dunkin Donuts on her way in, and we have—"

"No." I even shake my head, feeling the bandage pull at new skin. It will hurt for hours now. "No. Please."

We went for doughnuts the morning of the fire. I had stayed the night at Julie's, and Steve and Bob came over early.

"What's wrong with you, Julie? No eggs, no bread, no juice—how did you plan to feed us breakfast?" Bob faked rage, peering into her refrigerator.

"I didn't." She yawned. "Didn't your mother teach you not to invite yourself over for meals?"

"No. But I bet Lori will help me find something to eat, while Ms. Hostess of the Year ponders her sins."

We drove to Kroger's. It was a clear day, bright in spite of the snow on the ground. The wood-framed buildings of Julie's apartment complex slid by us. Bob put on sunglasses and we joked about Steve and Julie, in our absence, finally falling in love after all their years as friends.

"He'd be crazy, though, punkin. Julie may be pretty, but you're the nice one."

"Gee, thanks. That's just what every girl wants to hear."

I looked in the mirror on the sun visor. My hair was sticking up, and I had a hole in my Northwestern sweatshirt.

"Did I put my foot in my mouth?"

"Forget it."

Bob parked his Mustang. In the grocery, we studied the rows of doughnuts in the bakery section: powdered sugar, glazed, creme-filled, jelly-filled, iced, nonpareil-covered, twists, dunking sticks. I remember each one vividly; that might as well have been the last moment of my life. The glass case threw back a dim reflection of my face, but I looked beyond, deciding between blueberry and strawberry-filled doughnuts.

The nurse's aide and my food are gone. Someone is knocking at my door.

"Come in," I mutter, hoping whoever it is cannot hear me.

But Rick Simms, the man from the next hospital room over, rolls his wheelchair in. He worked for the electric company, and burnt his feet off fixing wires after a storm. He has a crazy quilt of grafted skin exposed up and down what remains of his legs. They say he's well enough to go home, but his wife doesn't want him anymore. I don't know if it's true.

"You've been quiet today. Just wanted to make sure you were still among the burned and living."

"What? You haven't heard my screams of anguish? My shrieks of unspeakable agony?"

The first week I kept Rick awake with my screaming. I don't remember if it was from the nightmare or the pain.

"Gosh, I forgot—my new earplugs! That must be why I don't hear you anymore."

"I'll have to try to scream louder," I say.

Rick laughs. Above the hospital gown, his face is unscarred. His brown beard fades into pale but healthy skin.

"Do you ever—you know—miss your feet?" I ask.

"Oh, no! Did something happen to them?" He clowns at peeking sideways, around the wheels of the chair, to empty space.

"No, I mean it. I miss my face today. I don't remember what it looked like. I want it back."

"That's not how you've always looked? Isn't gauze just the fashion nowadays?"

"Rick, stop it. Be serious."

He looks away from me.

"Okay. I miss my feet. I dream sometimes that they're still there, that I'm running. I cry when I wake up, and I want to yell horrible things at everyone. Then Angie or one of the other nurses comes in, and I figure it's not their fault. I make stupid jokes with them, I laugh with you, I visit other patients. But all I want is my feet back, and my old legs. And my wife."

His face is red. He's breathing too fast.

"I'm sorry," I say.

The words are meaningless. Rick and I stare at each other

for a minute. I can hear the traffic on the street outside: people driving to meetings or the grocery or just anywhere they want to go. The noise is distant.

"Plastic surgery does marvelous things, now," he says. "They're more careful with faces than legs, so maybe you—"

"No. They've told me. They say I should be realistic." I say the word carefully, suddenly finding it hard to pronounce.

Rick nods. He does not tell me that appearance doesn't matter, that I haven't really changed, that I'm lucky to be alive.

"They try to help," he finally says.

"Yes."

He rolls his wheelchair back into the hall. I wish suddenly that he had said what everyone else says. I might have believed him.

Of course, it is true: I'm lucky to be alive. The explosion was big, impressive. It made the papers, and for a while, before I returned to consciousness, I was a big celebrity. They interviewed Julie, Steve and Bob, even called my parents in Pittsburgh.

I have not read the stories. I do not want to. I remember it the way it happened.

When Bob and I got back to Julie's parking lot, Steve was leaning over the hood of her Honda, messing with wires.

"Beauty queen decided she had to take a shower before she could spend even a minute more with us," he said. "Somehow she decided that meant I would be perfectly happy to play mechanic for her."

"For this you're getting a master's in engineering?" Bob asked.

"Practical application skills."

"What's wrong?" I asked.

"Strange noises, a little whining when the car starts—it means nothing to me," he said.

"Have a doughnut—it might inspire you," I said.

Steve pulled a sugared doughnut from the box I offered him. Bob grabbed his third.

"Aren't you going to save any for Julie?" I asked.

"She's not here to make me, is she?"

"I was afraid you'd think that."

I took the box inside. Julie met me at the door.

"Has Steve fixed my car yet?"

"He's probably going to recommend a second opinion."

She giggled. I felt droplets from her wet hair as she slipped past me.

I think I smelled the gas then. At least, I felt a little strange, a little confused. Shouldn't I have given Julie a doughnut? I could hear everyone outside, laughing. She was pretty; I'd be nice.

I went to the kitchen and pulled down a pink and white china plate for the doughnuts. I stacked them, licking my finger when a curl of chocolate icing clung to it. Through the white-curtained window, I could see the other three outside. Julie rolled a snowball with her gloves and threw it at Steve. It slipped harmlessly down his back. Steve turned around, grinning. "Throw one at her," Bob yelled.

I decided to make hot water, for coffee or tea or cocoa for them. The burner didn't come on under the kettle, so I searched for matches to relight the pilot light.

When I struck the match, the world exploded.

I hit the window, felt it shatter behind me. Flames leaped around me, but I couldn't move. The orange and yellow hypnotized me. Then I stumbled, crashed sideways through the window frame.

I set the bushes on fire when I landed. I could smell my sweats burning, see the flames coming out the window. It was forever before Bob yanked me out of the bushes and rolled me over and over in the snow.

The whole time, I could hear Julie screaming on every side of me.

"You awake?" Julie walks into my room unannounced.

I blink. I haven't been asleep, but I'm confused. Julie is wearing a bright yellow wool suit; she must have come straight from work.

162

"Is it five already?"

"Time flies when you're having—sorry. No, it's only three. I left work early. Since it's Friday, I wanted to come over here before, uh, happy hour."

"Oh."

She smiles apologetically.

Suddenly I think of myself at four or five, taken to visit my grandmother. She never left her bed. Each visit, I squirmed in my chair in her dim, stuffy room, trying to avoid my parents' glares. It was a relief each time they finally let me go outside and play on her porch swing. It was a relief when she died.

"You didn't have to come today," I tell Julie. "You were just here Wednesday."

"Well—I wanted to." She smiles again, even more feebly. "Oh, here's your mail. The nurse gave it to me on the way in."

She tosses a couple letters on the bed. When I don't pick them up, she remembers I can't. She opens them for me.

"Here's a card from Bob. I remember Steve said he was going to Phoenix or San Francisco or someplace on business."

The card makes a joke about hospital Jell-o. Bob wrote nothing in it, just signed his name.

"He must be really busy," Julie says. "I mean, we've barely seen him since the fire."

She knows Bob hasn't come to visit me. But she moves on to the next envelope.

"Here's another letter from Lyle, with all your kids' signatures. The substitute teacher added a note, asking how you dealt with that ornery Jason Howard—"

"Jason? I never had any trouble." But I can barely remember his face, just the freckles and blue eyes.

"And here's something from your school superintendent." Her eyes scan the letter. "I guess they need to know if you will be able to return this year or if they should hire a replacement."

She holds out the letter for me to see.

"What are you going to do?"

"I have to think about it."

Julie nods.

"Would you be well enough?"

I shrug.

"I don't know if I want to go back." I don't tell her: elementary school children will always be scared of me now. I don't want to be the teacher all the kids pray they won't get.

"Well, with the settlement from the gas company, you won't need to for a long time. You have settled, haven't you?"

"No. They're paying my hospital bills, but—"

"Lori! The sooner you do it, the more you get, because it's all fresh in their minds and they're more afraid you'll sue."

We've talked about this before. It only depresses me. I say nothing.

"Now you'll probably have to go through a long lawsuit. I had my dad negotiate with them the day after the fire, and you know I had a lot left over after I bought new furniture and stuff. I'm probably going to buy a condominium now."

"Lucky you." I cannot help it. My voice is bitter. I try to sound friendlier. "Where have you been staying since the fire, anyway?"

"Well, Steve said he had extra room, so—"

I see it in her eyes.

"You two are more than friends now, right? This all *helped* you."

"Lori, don't be mad. I didn't want to tell you because it's not fair, I know it's not fair, but it's not my fault. I didn't make the gas leak. I didn't—"

"Light the match? Is it my fault?"

"No." She is crying. "No."

But she gets up every morning, looks in the mirror and rejoices that it didn't happen to her. I know it. And I know that it would never happen to her: her life is charmed. Mine is not. That's why I went for the safe things: the schoolteaching, the Lyle, Indianas, of the world, the place behind Julie in our circle of friends. I wanted more, but I shouldn't have.

164

"There's Kleenex in the drawer over here," I say, at last.

She pulls one out neatly, without tearing it. I watch her dab her eyes and blow her nose.

"I'm sorry. I'm glad for you and Steve," I lie. "Really."

"You are? You aren't mad?"

She starts to hug me, but I pull away.

"It would hurt," I say.

"I forgot."

We look away from each other. She glances at her watch and jumps up.

"Can you believe how late it is? I knew I wouldn't have much time. Steve and the others—friends from work—are going to be upset if I don't get there soon—"

"You should go, then." I try to smile.

She picks up her briefcase and walks away from my bed. At the door, she turns around.

"I'll tell Steve how great you're being about all this. He worries."

"Tell him not to."

Julie is already gone.

I relax, ready to feel sorry for myself. But the anger I held in has evaporated. I feel nothing.

The traffic outside is even quieter now. I hear one horn honking, then nothing. It is getting dark, and the shadows are reclaiming the corners of my room.

I try to picture Steve and Julie's work friends waiting for her in the bar. I imagine the warmth of the room, the jokes flowing around the wooden table, the way Julie will look as she weaves her way through the potted plants to her friends. Steve will search for an extra chair for her, and there will be more jokes.

It's all a mirage to me. Only gauze and silence are real.

I lie still, thinking about what I had before the fire. It wasn't so bad. I stare at the cards on the wall; if I can pick out the loop of Lisa Myers's handwriting, the tilt of Jimmy Hickson's, I can have it all back. But they are too far away.

I close my eyes and wait for the fire.

ELLEN KANNER

Skim Milk

I'VE BEEN SPENDING too many days inside again. It's time for Fumi to come collect me and take me to the garden at Meiji Shrine. We go there frequently, so we can mark changes in the garden and pond throughout the year, see the irises in spring, the chrysanthemums in autumn. The path from the entrance is pebbled, and we teeter in high heels, lean on each other for balance, and laugh. Fumi laughs more than giggles. Most Japanese women giggle, giggle and gasp at once, at some unseen embarrassment. Fumi has lovely teeth, like seed pearls. I want to tell her this, but it would make her shy. I have to watch what I say, can't say what I think. That is a problem here.

Fumi takes me to Meiji when I get like this, too closed up. I am anxious to see her, we haven't gotten together for our visits since last month. She's been busy, not working, but thinking. Fumi is thinking of divorcing her husband, Kitazawa-san, and I hope she does it. I have nothing against the man. I've never met him. Fumi, like me, is twenty-five. Her husband is a dozen years older than she is, which might not make a difference in a marriage based on love, but theirs was an arrangement.

In an attempt to become more familiar with the Western culture she does not comprehend, Fumi reads contemporary American and English novels. She is fluent in English language, but not Western thought. I tell her I can't help her, I don't understand it, either. She'll look at me with a glint of hardness in those dark eyes. She should be happy with what she has, most Japanese women are, but Fumi has read too many books, seen too many foreign movies, seen too much of the love between my husband and me. She has been seduced by what she has learned.

Fumi was my language teacher before she was my friend. I hired her three weeks after my husband moved to Tokyo from the States. He wanted to do everything for me, wanted my days here to slip away like drops of bath oil in warm water. He hadn't considered the loneliness I felt when he went off for work every day. I felt like Rapunzel, young, lovely, and shut away in a tower. I had learned a smattering of Japanese, all the niceties, but they were meaningless, because when our neighbors asked questions, I couldn't understand or answer them.

Some of my husband's co-workers told me about this woman, Fumi-san, who would come to your house and give Japanese lessons. They said she was patient and efficient. I envisioned a cross between Madame Butterfly and Tojo. I dressed up for my first lesson. So did she. She arrived wearing a pastel polka-dot dress, and heels more high than comfortable. There was a little lacy ribbon in her hair. She looked like a wind-up doll. I poured tea and we talked. I did everything wrong, misused the few words I knew. She was anxious to grasp what I tried to say. We both came away feeling I'd need a lot of work.

I told my husband I didn't know if Fumi-san could work out. She was what everyone had said, but she seemed so stiff. I told him my project was to make Fumi-san laugh. Laughter is my tool of seduction. At least, it used to be. Fumi-san didn't laugh at our next lesson. She smiled some. We talked about ourselves in English and Japanese. One week, she looked at our honeymoon pictures. She did not have with her a picture of her husband, who is a bank manager, and, she said, rather fat.

At the end of the following lesson, Fumi-san produced her own wedding photographs. She looked the same in the pictures, smiling the same tight, solicitous smile. That was when she said theirs was an arranged marriage. When I went to pay her, she bowed deeply from the waist, and said she could no longer ask for money, because she was getting as much out of the lessons as I was. I tried to insist, but she got offended, as any Japanese will do, if you press money on him. So Fumi's visits continued once a week, sometimes more frequently, but without the structure of a class. She still corrects my Japanese, as Lord knows, she will always have to do.

After Fumi and I go to Meiji, we may walk along Omote-sando, where the students hang out. I'll drag Fumi into one of the boutiques, and put something absurd on her. Last time, it was a lime green coat with leopard trim. Not bad on her, really. Or we'll go to one of the coffee houses right on the street. Fumi likes to be coaxed into ordering pastries, and eats them moaning in ecstasy. I drink Suntory, Japanese whiskey. It's hard to get other drinks here, aside from beer, for which I never developed a taste. If Fumi is feeling good about leaving her husband, I'll order coffee and whiskey, and drink them together, a sip of one, then the other. It's enough to blow the top of my head off. We'll watch people come and go. Everyone watches each other on Omote-sando. The girls are so frilly and pretty, the boys preen and fluff up their hair, arranged in impractical coifs. I like to watch them now, while they're young, before they are pressed for good and forever into the Japanese Mold.

There is something of the lemming in every Japanese, a desire to pursue pointless goals—well, pointless by American standards, which are all I know. Fumi's husband works as a manager in one of the many branches of Fuji Bank. He is an upper-level employee, and puts in an average of sixty hours a week there. He does not hope to earn overtime for such devotion. He does not anticipate promotion anytime soon. He works that hard to keep his job. He is afraid if he worked a standard work week, he would be fired for not showing more initiative. He works all day, every day but Sunday. Sundays, he wants to do nothing but sleep, for which one cannot blame him. He prefers not to go out evenings. He takes Fumi out for dinner on her birthday, if she hints at it sufficiently in advance. They take no vacations. They go days without speaking, not from anger, but from this state of coexistance. This is the rule with Japanese couples, rather than the exception. Fumi deserves better.

One time, I risked a cultural blunder. "You don't mind it being like this—with you and your husband?"

She smiled and bowed her head, spreading her hands. This is a common Japanese gesture, which means we must accept things as they are. This is why so many Japanese can crowd into subway cars. It is not for us to complain. This is how it is.

I have been a sinister influence on her, but I didn't mean to be. I have worried for Fumi, because I see her life mapped out as clearly as if she was a character in one of the subversive books I lend her. Fumi will have children. A Japanese wife has no status until she does. Her husband will never spend time with them, never have the time to spend. He will take weekend trips with his friends, and board a bullet train for Kyoto, wearing a loud checkered sport coat, a bottle of Suntory whiskey in hand, and drink for the whole three-hour trip, arriving sodden and soused, happy to be without his family. Fumi will stay at home with the children, tending their needs, neglecting her own. She will put away the pretty doll clothes she wears, and adopt a more mature style, even before she turns thirty. She will become bitter and fretful when her children grow up and find interests outside the home. She will come to feel superfluous and unfulfilled.

I face a similar destiny, and face it now, because I cannot have children. I am empty, I am sterile. My husband and I have talked it over till I don't want to anymore. We now wear false faces and tell each other how lucky we are, because we will forever be on our honeymoon. I don't tell him I think of us as two figures atop a wedding cake, unreal, frozen in time. I feel I am carrying death around in my womb every day. My Japanese doctor briskly suggests I get over this emotionalism and get on with life. He gave me those tests, he told me I couldn't have children. But carry on, he says, do not allow yourself to become depressed. He wears bow ties. His eyebrows arch up high. I close my eyes and see his face, fleshy and clownlike.

It's not pity I want. I got more than I cared for from my mother and sisters and friends, smug in their own fecundity, femininity. What I want is a long, voluptuous cry, without having to worry if it will upset my husband or cause the neighbors to speculate about us, strange foreigners that we are. Ever since we found out, about me being infertile, I mean, I've had to be the good Japanese, to get on with it, as my doctor says. There hasn't been the luxury of tears. Crying makes Fumi uneasy. She says when she's upset, she talks to her mother, but only if the problem doesn't concern the family. It is shameful to speak ill of one's husband, or to cause one's family to lose face. I want to put my head on Fumi's shoulder and soak her clever little designer dresses with tears.

My husband wanted a child more than I did, I think. So I can't be too sad when he is here, because his feelings are still so close to the surface. He looks at the beautiful Japanese children and at me, as though I cheated him, as though I wanted to. He doesn't know he looks at me that way, or he wouldn't do it. I've tried crying alone in the apartment, but there's no comfort in it. Fumi wants to do for me all she can, I know that. That's the reason behind these interminable treks, to the museums, to lunch, to Kabuki, and to Meiji.

I am dressed and ready, which is rare. Fumi is late. She missed the connecting train. She asks how I am, without looking me in the eye. I tell her I am better. I lie. It is the Japanese thing to do.

Fumi and I are the same size, but she maintains an aura of

fragile petiteness, and I feel big and tough as a horse, in comparison. Her skin is smooth and powdered to perfection. I want to touch her, as I once longed to touch my mother's fragile Dresden figurines. They surprised me, the bisque porcelain scratched rather than soothed. Fumi's hands are that way, small, but stubby-fingered, with chewed, ragged nails. She does not wear polish, because it would draw attention to her hands. My hands are soft and cool, the nails spatulate and lacquered with Shisiedo polish. Worry doesn't show on them.

Fumi says it's cool out, and windy, but I've anticipated that. I wonder how the pretty park greenery survives the smoggy air and harsh Tokyo climate. Winter days here are brilliant, and looking out from the inside, I could believe it was a balmy day. I have learned—the clearer the day, the colder the temperature. There's a line from *The Mikado*, "things are seldom what they seem / Skim milk masquerades as cream." Gilbert and Sullivan knew the Japanese.

The garden at Meiji Shrine in February is still in winter shock. I don't see any carp in the pond. Fumi says they have gone to where the water flows. Where we are, it is still, brown, and frozen in patches. She has brought a camera, she wants to take a picture. It is true the Japanese commemorate any event with photographs. The grass is dun-colored, the ground is hard. I sit for her and smile in my black coat, hat and sunglasses. All that can be seen of me is my mouth, a cupid's bow of red lipstick. I think of the Cheshire Cat from *Alice in Wonderland.* That was one of my favorite stories as a girl. I won't have a daughter to read it to.

I agree with the Japanese doctor, I should get over dwelling on "my problem," or so he calls it. I will be able to, in time, but now it's a bruise I wake up with every morning, sensitive to the touch. I think about this, and Fumi is thinking, too. She was quiet on the subway ride over. I don't blame her, but I wish she would tell me what's happened. Kitazawa-san must be humiliated. And angry. None of her family will take her in, if she leaves him. Her parents will say she is ungrateful and selfish, interested only in her own happiness, as if that was a crime.

I am becoming cold, even in my winter coat, but I won't say anything. Fumi does not understand how I can be so affected by winter weather. I think she sees it as some weakness in my character. I don't know why we came today. The trees aren't dead, but they are in a deep sleep. No busload of tourists has come to make a pilgrimage to Meiji Shrine. Our only company is a flock of crows, glossy-feathered, cruel-eyed, cawing.

Fumi shudders. "Maybe you would like some coffee or something," she says, "maybe we should get out of this wind."

We do. We seek refuge in an Italian-y looking coffee shop with fake black marble floor and table tops. The crowd of students has already assembled. They wear their sunglasses inside, and take up the tables closest to the street. It is small and steamy, and smells of cigarette smoke and women wearing Poison.

I order coffee without the whiskey. Something is wrong, I can tell. Fumi orders a bowl of spaghetti. I ask her what she has been doing.

She smiles a smile which conceals more than it reveals. She asks what I mean.

All this playacting would be most annoying with a friend from the States, but the Japanese have a fixed etiquette, and I obey the rules. My voice is neutral as I ask, "Have you decided to leave your husband?"

Fumi and I establish eye contact. The lanky waiter delivers our orders in silence, smiles, and departs. Fumi says, "No."

I do not touch her sad hand, lying on the table. She does not liked to be touched. "Why? What's wrong, Fumi?"

"You can congratulate me," she says. "I am going to have a baby."

"Oh, God," I say, and amend that with, "how wonderful."

She smiles and shrugs, "My family is pleased. They say it is

time I have a child. They say it will make me a more respon-
sible person. But I cannot leave my husband now. I cannot go
against everything. It is too hard."

I want to punch her in the stomach, in her fecund womb,
bearing life. She eats her spaghetti, slurping up the noodles.
"Why not now? It's the best time. Leave him before the baby,
you can both make a new start. You could stay—you could
stay with us." I'd have the baby, Fumi, please let me have the
baby.

"We have reached an understanding," she says, and dabs
her mouth on a paper napkin the size of a postage stamp. "I
will not interfere with his life, but he will provide for us. That
is his job. That is a husband's role."

"What about you? You want to become like—like that?" I
point to a passing matron, made old before her time, living
on scraps of affection, fearing the time her children will
move away, and she will be alone.

Fumi looks away. "It has been decided. It will not be possible for us to see each other so often, then," she says, and
doesn't have to say why. Kitazawa-san can hardly want his
wife and bearer of his child to be under the influence of evil
Western thought. And I won't want to spend much time with
someone who has what I lack.

"No," I say, "of course not." My coffee is cold.

"You understand, then?" She wants to leave. So do I.

I nod. She reaches for the check. This time, I let her take
it.

"I am sorry," Fumi says, "I hope things will become happy
for you."

I smile, bow my head, spread my hands. I accept this. This
is how it is.

CARY   CATHARINE   HOLLADAY

Dry Ice

THE THERAPY GROUP met once a week at an old brick church. The group leader, Bill Hatcher, liked to read the tombstones. His favorite one said, "Gone to be an Angel." On nice days, the group sat under a huge sycamore tree that dated back to the Civil War, when the church had served as a hospital for troops injured in battles around Memphis. Bill had seen photographs of the tree in its early years, surrounded by convalescent Confederates. Memphis had grown, but this was still just an old church in a tiny country town, ringed by stubbly fields and tangled woods.

Bill Hatcher was six-foot-four, swaybacked and lean, his hair just beginning to gray. He knew that his overbite kept him from being handsome. Once, he had been sure he would be a basketball player. He had never intended to become a counselor, but it was the only job where people seemed to like him. He had been fired from his previous positions in publishing houses. He hadn't done anything wrong in the publishing houses, but always the boss would find some reason to let him go.

Now he worked at a county mental health clinic, and every Tuesday afternoon at 5:00, he came here. Because it was the church his parents belonged to, he felt he couldn't refuse to counsel the members, even though no money was offered. The preacher himself, a young man just out of the seminary, was in the group, along with a heavy-set brunette seamstress named DeeDee; a quiet, catlike, one-eyed meter-reader named Ralph; and an older couple, Mr. and Mrs. Cousins, who had a consignment store that sold second-hand clothing, furniture, and tools. And there was Laura Guard, whom Bill loved. She ran a doll shop.

The previous week, a cicada had come and perched on top of the "Gone to be an Angel" tombstone and had proceeded slowly, slowly, to step out of its old skin, dry its new wings, and fly away. There was excited discussion about how appropriate that was, for the cicada to come and do that while everyone here was pondering how to make changes, how to be happy.

Now a leaf, tinged with yellow, fell into Bill's lap as he sat beneath the tree on a hassock and watched everyone gather in a circle around him. Laura Guard came and sat beside him. She wore a billowing khaki dress, and despite the heat there was a pumpkin-colored scarf wound around her neck and fastened with a pink rhinestone honeybee pin. Her fingers played with the fringe of the scarf. Bill loved her because she was so gentle. She had been hurt in so many ways that the anger was flushed out of her and only the gentleness remained. Her husband had left her, her young son had died in a car crash. She spoke little at the group meetings. Bill suspected that she was still in love with her husband, even though, as far as he knew, they had divorced and she never heard from him anymore. Bill had tried, shyly and without success, to get her to sign up for regular private therapy. He believed it would help her.

Now she picked a wilted leaf off the ground and smiled, "Always in August, you tell yourself it's just the heat making them yellow, but fall's on the way."

"There's those that won't complain," mumbled Ralph. As usual, he smelled of gasoline.

"Pardon?" said Laura, and Ralph fairly screamed his same reply.

Everyone was there. It was the Cousins' turn to bring refreshments, and Mrs. Cousins passed around paper cups and an open cooler brimming with sweet chartreuse liquid in which a fly floated. Ralph sipped his, then spat it out and poured the rest of his cupful on the ground. Bill wanted to do likewise, but of course he couldn't. Mrs. Cousins glared balefully at Ralph.

"Who'd like to go first today?" asked Bill, making his voice consciously mild, sensing tension. There was a long silence, broken only by the sounds of a man mowing the field next to them. Bill looked out at that field, deep with golden shadows. His gaze wandered to the church marquee, which sat just outside the front door and bore the name of the preacher and the time of the Sunday service. Every week, the preacher arranged the plastic letters to spell out a proverb, a saying, or a threat. This week the marquee said, "You think it's hot up *here*?"

As the silence stretched out, Laura Guard ran a hand up under her hair, stroking her scalp. It was her habit. By the end of the hour, she would have drawn her hand through her hair many times. Whether her hair was blondish or a sort of tarnished silver, Bill couldn't decide. She must be over forty, he knew, a decade older than he was, yet when he looked at her, years fell away and she could have been a twenty-year-old girl by a swimming pool. She was slender, but she hid her figure in billows and pleats; her hands were smooth as soap and her cheekbones, though sharp, were not bitter. But ten years older. He imagined what his mother would say, if she knew of his feelings: "Why, she was already halfway grown when you were still swinging on the moon."

"I'd like to start," the preacher burst out, and everyone looked at him. He seemed ready to cry. He had a high, braying voice, made more strident when he was upset. "I didn't pass my Presbytery exam again, and now I'll have to face the elders and see if they want to keep me on or let me go."

"Of course they'll keep you, Doug," said DeeDee, leaning forward in her lawn chair. Her eyebrows formed an inverted V of concern; her silo-shaped breasts pressed against her blouse. The blouse had little metallic threads in it, Bill saw.

"No they won't!" barked the preacher. A horsefly clung to his thin arm, and he swatted at it in fury. "That exam was damned hard, and now I've failed it two times. It's not, 'What was up in the sky on Christmas?' and 'Who was Mary?' It's real difficult stuff."

"Well," began Mrs. Cousins, "since it's public knowledge that you earn $26,000 a year, and only work one day a week, I'd've thought the least you could do was pass some test."

In the shocked silence, Bill reflected that the preacher's jeans must have come from the boys' department; they didn't fit right, although he was so short and thin. Bill bore the preacher no ill will, but he couldn't help but agree, secretly, with Mrs. Cousins. He was amazed that the church had set such a high salary, and he could tell that Doug just read his Sunday sermons out of books.

"It's not your job to criticize him!" cried DeeDee to Mrs. Cousins.

"Somebody has to," Mrs. Cousins replied briskly, pouring herself more of the green drink. Her round, dangling earrings reminded Bill of eyeballs. "First we heard about how scared he was to have taken this job. Then we heard about how nervous he was before the test. Now he's failed it—again. He has to realize that if he puts his mind to it, he can pass that test, and then maybe he'll start deserving all that money. As it is now, he's not allowed to do weddings and funerals, so we still have to pay somebody else to—"

"It's all money with you," said the preacher. "And you too, DeeDee!" Unexpectedly he attacked his ally. "I earn my money, more so than any of you'd admit, anyhow."

Ralph chuckled. "I've got one for you, Doug. How many wise men were there?"

To stem the tide of torment, Bill hastily interposed.

"Would everyone take a pencil and paper, and we're going to do something new." His hand touched Laura's as he passed pencils around. Laura's fingers were cool. The preacher's face and neck were scarlet.

"Self-portrait," said DeeDee, making a mark and holding her paper up for the group to see. She had drawn a big circle. DeeDee had always been heavy, and now she was pregnant. Her problem, she had told the group weeks earlier, was that she did not want the baby. She had wanted it at first, when she thought the baby's father was going to marry her, but he had left town, and now she was six months along, all by herself.

"Aww, DeeDee," said Mrs. Cousins. She snatched the paper and drew exaggerated eyes on it, with long lashes. "Your lovely eyes."

DeeDee smiled shakily. Forgiveness was in the air, for what Mrs. Cousins had said about Doug. At least, DeeDee had forgiven her, but Doug, who sat with his head averted, had not.

"Actually, we're not doing self-portraits today," said Bill, disturbed by the sarcasm in his voice. "I thought we could make lists of the things that frighten us, and talk about that." Bill repeated his role to himself: find out what a person truly wants, and then help him identify specific steps toward achieving it. This tactic, the list of fears, was something the head counselor at the clinic had suggested to Bill and other staff members as a technique for helping people get to know themselves. Bill had tried it before with individual patients, finding that the more they talked, the less he had to do. But an inner voice said, It's just a trick, like getting them to make paper swans.

"Things—that—scare—us," said Mr. Cousins slowly, writing the words at the top of his paper. "Not us. Me!" No one laughed. It was typical of what he would say. He was so much in his wife's shadow that people paid him little attention.

Mrs. Cousins joked, "We used to be afraid our crabapple trees would be all eaten up by mealybugs, but I put some cut white potatoes nearby, and now the bugs go to the taters instead."

Pencils scratched on paper. Ralph took off one shoe, held it on his lap, and used the sole as a surface to write against. Mrs. Cousins ticked her tongue. The preacher sat with his arms folded, not writing. Laura Guard bent over her list; Bill could not read her face. He never forgot she was there, though the others just talked around her.

While they wrote, Bill pondered his own fears, fears that multiplied like mealybugs. He was afraid of so many things: of never getting married, of not making enough money, of the future, of losing his parents. He was afraid of feeling lonely or frantic or just blue, because he felt that way so often, and each time it happened, it was terrible. He was afraid of being thought badly of. He remembered a girl who used to live in his apartment building. She was cute, he'd thought she liked him. She'd invited him in for brownies, and before he knew it, he'd eaten the whole plate of them, not leaving a single one for her, all the while talking about his job search. She looked disgusted. Her face clearly said, "Hog!" That was the way it always was with women—his titanic insecurity. He couldn't be himself around them.

Except maybe with Laura, in his dreams. He felt protective toward her. She was the kind of person that even a wild rabbit would let come up and pet it.

"Things that scare you," Bill began, breaking the silence. "Scare you, frighten you, shock you, unnerve you. Talking about them will help. Let's start with DeeDee, at my left, and go around the circle."

DeeDee crossed her legs at the knee and swung her foot nervously. "So many things scare me, I don't hardly know where to begin. Mainly this kid. I'm afraid that after it's born, I won't be happy anymore. I'm afraid that it won't have a good life growing up. I'm afraid I'll never see Rodney, the baby's father, again, and that I won't ever have any more boyfriends."

Mr. Cousins cleared his throat and said, "Young, pretty girl like you! Loads of men would be proud to marry you." Mrs. Cousins turned her head and goggled at her husband.

DeeDee burst into tears. "So why didn't Rodney? He said

he loved me. Said it the day the mall gave away free ice cream. There was a child's plastic swimming pool set up in front of Woolworth's, a pool all filled with ice cream sundaes, and while we were eating ours, Rodney said he loved me. And then he left. But that's not all I feel bad about. Dr. Brenner said it might be twins."

Mr. Cousins said, "Then I have just the thing for you—a double-wide stroller our daughter-in-law wants to get rid of." He held his hands wide apart as if measuring. "When you walk down the street, everybody'll move aside for you. They'll have to!"

Magically, DeeDee's tears dried. She looked at Mr. Cousins with hope.

Mrs. Cousins shifted in her chair. "I'm next. Now, Woody here always says I'm shy," and she patted her husband's leg, "and the truth is, I have more fears than anybody else I know. Some days, I get nervous just wondering what to fix for supper! Why should that be? Whatever I fix is okay with Woody." Mr. Cousins nodded emphatically. "And I worry about the pains in my joints and this feeling in my chest like somebody put a firecracker in it. I'm diabetic," she said importantly, "and I worry about getting AIDS. The needles I use are the throw-away kind, but what if a person with AIDS works at the needle factory and uses one, just to be mean? But mostly I worry about bad gossip. I've always been real careful about my reputation, always been scared somebody would say something about me that wasn't true. I know no one here would do that," and she swept the circle slowly with her small eyes. "We're all good Christians." She fixed Ralph with a concentrated frown.

Bill said, "Everything we say here is confidential, Mrs. Cousins, but now is a good time to reassure ourselves that nothing we say here ever goes beyond this group."

"Not beyond the shade of this sycamore tree," murmured Laura, and Mrs. Cousins regarded Laura, then the tree, with suspicion, as if the branches concealed dozens of scribbling reporters.

"If anybody says anything bad about Fanny, they'll have to

answer to me," said Mr. Cousins primly. (Bill thought Laura smiled at this, but he wasn't sure). "*My* number one fear is losing my wife. Every day I pray the Lord will see fit to make the diabetes go away."

Mrs. Cousins bridled at this, beaming. Then her face changed. "And we're afraid the store mascot, our parrot, Tut-Tut, might die," she added, as if amending a prayer. "He keeps pecking at his feet."

Bill checked his watch, wondering why he ever worried about filling up the hour. Certain group members were so very talkative that he often had to cut them short.

"My wife and Tut-Tut, they're my life," said Mr. Cousins. He pulled at his beard, as short and evenly-trimmed as carpet fiber. "And our son and his wife and their two little boys, though they don't visit us as much as they ought to, and that breaks my heart and Fanny's too. But this is a list of things that scare you, and heartbreak's on another list."

It was Doug's turn. "Nuclear war. But maybe that would have a good side effect—people might start praying again." His small jaw was set as if to say, Bring on the bombs.

"Oh Doug, nobody thinks about nuclear war!" protested DeeDee.

Bill said nothing, realizing that he not only hated to talk about nuclear war, but that he disliked anyone who did. While the preacher lectured the group about radioactivity and its attendant dangers, Bill thought about Laura's doll shop. It was only a few blocks from his clinic, and when he walked past, he sometimes glimpsed her through the window, arranging the wide-eyed dolls on the shelves. They were old-fashioned creations, with snowy pinafores, jointed arms, and coils of glossy hair; their porcelain faces were serious, as if they led lives full of compelling truths. Once Bill had bought a doll there for his seven-year-old niece. It was a boy doll in a little suit of football clothes. The suit had tiny plastic shoulder pads, a red jersey, matching red breeches, and soft black plastic shoes that pulled on over the doll's stiff feet. "And little red socks," Laura had said happily. But Bill's niece disliked the doll, saying she preferred "regular pretty ones."

Bill realized that Doug was finished talking about war, and a restless silence prevailed. Bill thought he felt a raindrop on his forehead. He prompted, "Ralph?"

"My worry is more crucial than unwanted babies and nuclear war. It's the general trend toward rudeness in this country. I read an article about it."

"But *you* are rude, Ralph," challenged Mrs. Cousins. "Pouring my limeade on the ground!"

"Interruptions, for example." Ralph nodded at her, his good eye narrowed, his scent of gasoline strong. "One person breaking into the speech of another. That's the form of rudeness that people in a survey said they hated most of all."

"I wasn't interrupting!" said Mrs. Cousins. "It's just give-and-take in these sessions."

"Give and take, that's right," said DeeDee. "I think you're afraid to open up, Ralph."

While Ralph took out a handkerchief and blew his nose, Bill said, "Nobody has to open up more than they want to."

"Exactly," Ralph said. "Everybody's got problems. It's rude and selfish to complain all the time, and that in my opinion is what everybody here needs to learn. But since all of you-all are waving your dirty underwear in public, I'll give you something to think on. I'm afraid my garbage collector might stop coming. We had an argument about the way he leaves stuff all over the place—pieces of paper and tin cans and God knows what else that falls off his van. Yet he wants everything wrapped up tidy in plastic bags. I said, To hell with gift-wrapped garbage. So I taught him a lesson. When I heard his van coming, I had myself in my biggest can, with the lid over me. And then when he lifts off that lid, I jump out and yell at him and spit. Well, he hasn't come back, and now I've got so much garbage I'll have to take it to the dump myself." Dejectedly he motioned to his pickup truck in the parking lot. "Loaded up before I came."

DeeDee and Mrs. Cousins clamored, "Serves you right!" Doug piped up, "If that's our big worry, would you like some of mine?" Mr. Cousins rumbled, "I've never had any trouble with *my* garbage man. He's like a member of the family."

Laura was laughing, softly at first, then harder, her hands over her mouth, rocking back and forth. It was the first time Bill had seen her laugh like this, and he was enthralled. He, too, laughed, out of pure joy. Then Mr. Cousins was saying, "Hey, it's raining," and the preacher said, "Our time's up," and in truth it was raining, drops spattering down through the jade leaves of the sycamore tree, and there was the strong headwind of a thunderstorm, blowing their skirts and pantlegs hard against their knees.

"What are you scared of, Laura?" demanded DeeDee, folding her plastic chair flat.

"Being struck by lightning," Laura cried.

Mrs. Cousins' hair, layered in an artichoke style, stood up in the wind. She touched Laura's shoulder. "You be careful this week, girl. Last night I had a bad dream about you. I dreamed you died."

The group scattered, each person with a lawn chair under his arm, Ralph loping back to his laden truck, the Cousinses hurrying to their shiny new car, DeeDee setting off, flat-footed, to her house down the road, Doug scurrying back into the church. In seconds, Bill and Laura stood alone under the tree. Her face was blank and vulnerable, shellshocked, like the expressions of some of the sick Confederates in old photographs.

Love and pity welled up in Bill's heart. He said, "Don't pay one bit of mind to that ignorant old biddy."

"I'm glad I didn't get my turn." Her voice was rapid and light. She jerked the fringe of her scarf around her fingers. "I don't like to talk about fears. When my husband said, Let's stay married but see other people, I wondered, how can things go on as before? All kinds of innocent things became edged in awfulness, like a tuna sandwich on the kitchen counter or the feeling of blankets at night, everything turned into fear. And then a year later he left me. Even now I wonder what did I do to make him go away? Have you ever seen dry ice, Bill? Sometimes at picnics, people pack cold drinks in it."

183

He nodded, held by her amber-flecked eyes, his profes-
sionalism shattered by emotion.

"It changes from a solid into a gas, never going through the
liquid stage in between, and I wanted to be able to change
like that, to skip the middle stage, which is pain."

"You deserve all of the good, Laura, and none of the
bad."

"But I'm afraid the phone will ring. I'm afraid I won't
remember which way to turn out of this driveway to go
home. I'm a quiet person, and I like quiet things. I still hurt.
Once, I was away from my house for a long time and when I
got back, it was winter, and I found twenty dead birds in my
woodstove. They had flown down the flue to get warm, and
they had died because I'd failed to replace the screen over
the chimney. Are you afraid of anything, Bill?"

The wind shirred through the big tree. A blackbird sang a
short, distressed tune; thunder sounded. He would say it, he
would. He gathered his breath. "Of never getting to tell you
how much I admire you."

With two fingers, she brushed his cheek, and he stood so
still that his muscles were rock, or air. "It's all right," she
said.

He watched her turn and walk back to her car. He recalled
her telling him how she'd gone unnamed until her mother, a
telephone operator, decided one day to pick the tenth
female name that came up in person-to-person calls, and it
happened to be Laura. He watched while she tucked her
small body into her old car, turned on the ignition, and drove
down the hill and away, looking like one of her dolls behind
the wheel. Her taillights flashed in the rain.

The blackish fringe of the sycamore leaves flapped against
the sky. Bill collected the pencils and scraps of paper that lay
on the ground, the discarded lists of fears. He was surprised
that anyone had left their list behind. He would have hidden
such a list safely away. But he recognized Ralph's handwriting, and that of Mr. Cousins and DeeDee. Ralph had put,
"pickpockets." DeeDee said, "riding on trains." Mr. Cousins
had scrawled: "that there will be a wasp on the toilet seat

because I was stung there once." Every list said: losing my family, dying, getting sick or crippled, growing old, not having enough money.

He felt he had failed to help anyone today. He told himself, I should stop having these meetings. Next week, I'll tell them that that's the last time. Next week, or the week after that. He had, in fact, no idea about how to help the preacher overcome his fear of nuclear war or Mrs. Cousins her dread of catching AIDS. Or were those fears a kind of security for them, something to hang on to, to blame?

He asked himself, What do I want? and he imagined everyone in the therapy group—Mr. and Mrs. Cousins, DeeDee, Ralph, the preacher, Laura—all smiling, their mouths wide open, growing and changing, their homely human terrors resolved at last.

Passionately he wanted for Laura to come rolling back up the driveway in her rusty car, inviting him to supper. They could go anywhere, a fast-food chicken place, and she would be dreamy and kind, laughing the way she had laughed a short time before.

He waited, but she did not come, and after awhile, as the rain fell harder, he drove away.

Laura Leigh Hancock has won the Nicholson-Nielsen Careeer Award of the NSAL 1988 competition in short story; she was sponsored by the Birmingham Chapter of Alabama. After completing her Bachelor of Arts degree at Reed College, Oregon, she spent the next two years teaching English in Botswana in the United States Peace Corps. As winner of the Henry Hoyns Fellowship in fiction writing, she is at present completing a Master in Fine Arts at the University of Virginia. Author of the novel *The Second Firing*, she is also at work on a second novel based on her experiences in Africa. Currently, Ms. Hancock is teaching fiction writing at the University of Virginia, and "dreams of returning to a coffee farm on the Kona coast of Hawaii, spinning tales about people I've met and tending to coffee trees."

Carol Vivian Spaulding, winner of the Josephine Meray Heathcoate Foundation Award of the NSAL 1988 competition in short story, was sponsored by the Fresno Chapter of California. After receiving a Bachelor of Arts in English and a Master of Arts in Creative Writing from California State University, she entered the doctoral program at the University of Iowa. Author of a collection of seven short stories, she is recent winner of the American Association of University Women Graduate Fellowship, the Takolon Incentive Award, and the Sage Fiction Award. Last summer, Ms. Spaulding had the "mind-expanding experience" to be the ghost writer for a woman in France for six weeks. "Being a ghost writer is like being an actor. I have to prepare for a role and create it," she says. Whether it be on the university campus, traveling through Europe, or in Paris, France, she continues to write.

David Anthony Dobbs, winner of the Francesca Nielson Memorial Career Award in the NSAL 1988 competition in short story, was sponsored by the Champaign-Urbana, Illinois, Chapter. He is a native of Austin, Texas. After graduation from Oberlin College, Ohio, Mr. Dobbs has lived in New York, Connecticut, Texas, and Illinois. His non-fiction has appeared in the *Chicago Tribune,* the *Los Angeles Times,* and *Wildbird* and *Climbing* magazines. He now lives with his wife and two dogs in New Hampshire, where he is working as a freelance writer and writing a novel, of which "Placing Protection" is the first chapter.

Tina Marie Conway, winner of the Estelle Campbell Career Award of the NSAL 1988 Competition in short story, was sponsored by the North Florida Chapter in Tallahassee, Florida. A graduate of the University of Florida, she continued her education at the University of Colorado and Florida State University. Writer of fiction and poetry, she is published in *Black Ice, The Florida Review, Slipstream* and *Woodrider* among others. At present, Ms. Conway is living in Boulder, Colorado, writing a novel set in Battlecreek, Michigan, during World War II.

Young William Smith, Jr., is winner of the Dorothy and Bruce Strong Career Award in the NSAL 1988 competition in short story, and he was sponsored by the Little Rock, Arkansas, Chapter. A graduate of the University of Georgia with a Bachelor of Arts in English, Phi Beta Kappa, Mr. Smith is now completing a Master of Fine Arts in creative writing at the University of Arkansas. Currently, he is teaching English and Literature at the University, as well as serving as an Officer in the Army Reserve.

Marty Leslie Levine, winner of The Mame Doud Eisenhower Career Award in the NSAL 1988 competition in short story, was sponsored by the Pittsburgh, Pennsylvania, Chapter. A graduate of the University of Michigan, he recently completed a Master in Fine Arts in Fiction Writing from the University of Pittsburgh. Five of his articles have appeared in *The Pittsburgh Magazine* and in 1987 *The Pitts-*

burgh Magazine short story competition brought him honorable mention. Currently employed copyediting scientific research manuscripts, Mr. Levine is at work on a novel.

Renée Manfredi, winner of the Kurt Jungerkes Career Award in the NSAL 1988 competition in short story, was sponsored by the Bloomington, Indiana, Chapter. At present, she is completing a Master of Fine Arts Degree program at Indiana University. Her short stories have appeared in literary journals which include *Mississippi Review, Michigan Quarterly Review, Cimmarron Review, Carolina Quarterly,* and *Alaska Quarterly Review.* Ms. Manfredi is at work on a new short story collection.

Linda Miller, recipient of the NSAL 1988 Members-At-Large Career Award in short story, was sponsored by the Mid-Michigan Chapter. A graduate of the University of Michigan with a Bachelor of Arts in Philosophy, Ms. Miller won the University of Michigan's Avery Hopwood Award for Major Short Story in 1987. In 1988 she received a Roy Cowden Fellowship, while completing a Master in Fine Arts in creative writing. At present, she is teaching creative writing at the University of Michigan, finishing a short story collection and at work on her first novel. "I didn't grow up on a chicken farm as my story might suggest," she writes, "but I lived in a kibbutz in Israel for two years and worked with chickens."

Rebecca Ann Jorns, born in Heidelberg, West Germany, of a U.S. military family, is a graduate of James Madison University, magna cum laude. She is winner of the Sir Henry and Lady Bell Career Award in the NSAL 1988 competition in short story, sponsored by the Arizona Valley of the Sun Chapter. She is author of a collection of short stories, *Threads Too Short To Use,* and of poems which are published in *The English Journal* and *Scottsdale Progress.*

Currently at work on a novel, she says of this experience, "my writing has never made me feel quite so proud before."

Margaret Peterson Haddix, winner of the Peggy McNamara Brown Career Award in the NSAL 1988 competition in short story, was sponsored by the Indianapolis Chapter, Indiana. She is the recipient of the Greer-Hepburn Writing Award, Miami University, 1985–1986. Her poetry, essays and articles have been published in numerous university journals. As a reporter for the *Indianapolis News,* Ms. Haddix writes book reviews and articles. She is at work on her second novel as well as short fiction.

Ellen Kanner is the winner of the Beryl Pierce Career Award in the NSAL 1988 competition in short story, and was sponsored by the Boca Raton, Florida, Chapter. A native of Miami, Florida, she graduated from Bennington College with a Bachelor of Arts in Writing and Philosophy. In public relations, Ms. Kanner has written for the *Miami News,* the *Talent Times, Tequesta,* and the *Journal* of the South Florida Historical Association. Her novel, *Geographic Cure,* was written during the two years she lived in Japan. She has recently completed the script for an educational video, and at present is a representative for Screen Actors Guild.

Cary Catharine Holladay, winner of the Alice and William Leigh Career Award in the NSAL 1988 competition in short story, was sponsored by the Washington, D.C., Chapter. Ms. Holladay earned a Bachelor of Arts at the College of William and Mary, and a Master of Arts in English at Pennsylvania State University. The author's publications include short stories in *West Branch, Missouri Review, Inlet, Shore Writers Sampler,* and *Cimmarron Review,* and "News From China" in the Fall 1988 *Shore Writers Sampler.* At present, she is a lecturer in the Department of English and Languages,

University of Maryland Eastern Shore, co-editor of *Maryland Review*, and a member of the Eastern Shore Writers Association.